A Piece of Cake

Cecile Levin

Published by Muffin Press
muffinpress@gmail.com
www.muffinpress.co.za

© Cecile Levin 2014

ISBN 978-0-620-61057-5 (print)
ISBN 978-0-620-62260-8 (epub)
ISBN 978-0-620-62261-5 (mobi)

Edited by Biddy Greene
Illustrations and cover by James Berrangé
Typesetting and design by User Friendly, Cape Town
Set in New Baskerville BT 10 on 13.5 pt
Printed and bound by Fishwicks Printers, Durban

To David

for forty-four wonderfully happy years of marriage –
even the years when I was writing this book!

MY SPECIAL THANKS TO...

Biddy Greene, who took the term 'editor' to new heights. To her surprise, and my joy, Alison, Margie and Joey the cat took over a larger part of her life than she'd ever anticipated. Biddy's professionalism and dedication (whatever the hour, day or night), her insistence on nothing but the right word or phrase, her memories of those 'good old days', plus her sense of humour, enthusiasm and her enjoyment of coffee, made this a stimulating and hugely satisfying experience for me. Without Biddy's hard work this book would still be a mess of computer files!

Val Letcher, who, when visiting Durban in 2011 from Stratton on the Fosse in Somerset, read the first chapter over 'a cuppa and a little something', and from then on encouraged me all the way – gently but firmly – via Skype and email.

James Berrangé, for his wonderful illustrations, which brought the characters to life with just the right stroke of the pencil, and quirky humour. And for his seemingly limitless patience in accepting my constantly changing ideas. It's an amazing experience to see your characters appear on paper – rather than just in your imagination...

Jo-Anne Friedlander, who joined the team as designer and typesetter, accepting the many last minute changes with apparent equanimity. She added to *A Piece of Cake* her special ingredients – meticulous design skills and her own flavour of insight. And, not least, an appreciation of Joey!

Isabella Stengel, who urged – indeed demanded – in the nicest possible way, over numerous cups of caffé and biscotti, that I finish the book.

My family and friends, who listened patiently to the latest developments (and disasters) on the road to publication, and must have wondered if the tale would ever end – or whether it was all just another figment of my imagination...

And to all those who generously shared their delicious recipes with Alison... a big thank you.

ABOUT THE AUTHOR

Cecile Levin was educated at Girls' Collegiate School, Pietermaritzburg and studied music at the University of Cape Town and at the University of Natal. She has taught music at schools and tertiary institutions in Cape Town and Durban.

Cecile has been a writer, on and off, all her life. As a schoolgirl and student she wrote children's stories for the *Natal Witness* and the *Sunday Times*. She has published two books for young children: *Take Note*, a songbook, and *A Special Gift*, a musical play.

She and her husband, David, live in Durban. They have twin daughters and a son, seven grandchildren – and no cat!

~ ~ ~

Biddy (Bridget Ewer), Val (Fann) and I (Cecile Liefman) were schoolgirls together at Collegiate in Pietermaritzburg for only a few years. More than 'Forty Years On', Biddy and Val met on a tour bus in Syria.

Biddy and I then got together – with Wendy Fuggle (Anger), another Collegiate 'Old Gell' – over a prolonged tea in Cape Town. And, after hilarious wanderings down memory lane, Biddy agreed to edit what was to become *A Piece of Cake*.

Stormy Weather

'Yes, Margie, I *am* sorting out the mess in the cupboards.'
Alison raised her eyes heavenwards with extreme irritation.
'Yes, I *am* filling the black bags with stuff I've been hoarding
forever. And yes, I *have* read your list on decluttering!'

Each comment was pronounced with increased emphasis.
'In fact I'd better stop chatting and carry on throwing out
while I'm still in the mood! Ciao!' Alison replaced the receiver
before her sister could offer any more well-meaning but
unappreciated suggestions. With an operatic gesture she tossed
the neatly typed list into the already overflowing wastepaper
basket.

'Liar!' she muttered to herself. 'You haven't even started!' She drained the last drops of her breakfast tea and stoically dismissed the thought of another dose of caffeine. She glared at the empty boxes and black bags, waiting open-mouthed to devour the memories of her life. Margie was annoyingly right, as always. Alison resented Margie's elder sister act, more than acceptable in her first years at school, but not now that they were both grandmothers! Margie's second name should have been Conscience instead of Constance, she thought irreverently. Thank goodness she lives near enough for when I need her, but too far away for casual visits. Despite the distance, she could hear Margie's sharp tones clearly in her mind: 'You're moving in two months! Stop wasting time! Get on with it!'

Thank you, Margie! Anyone who hadn't experienced it could not appreciate the trauma of down-sizing on one's own. And for an emotional hoarder like herself it was almost impossible. How did you know that you wouldn't need whatever you'd just thrown out? She thought of the size of her new home and knew she'd have to be ruthless. 'So easy to say, so difficult to do,' she sighed...

Alison loved the comfy, old house where she and Mark had spent more than forty happy years. Well, she'd thought they were happy, until Mark had flown off 'to regain his lost youth' with Felicity (aka Floozy, to Alison) – who just happened to be his boss's daughter. She was barely older than their own daughters.

But what had really shocked Alison was the fact that she had been the last person to find out about it.

'I believe the owners are getting divorced and selling the house,' the confident-looking woman at the gate had explained. 'I'm an estate agent. May I come in and look around?'

How could she have been so gullible? The warning signs had all been there – the frequent late nights at the office, the out of town 'business' weekends (bonding indeed!) and the office functions that didn't include her. She'd naively thought that the business was economising in these financially difficult times. 'And I'm not even blonde!' she had wailed to her friend Pam. But Mark had always been a workaholic, so why should she have been suspicious?

Alison combed her fingers through her shoulder-length, blonde – originally mousy – hair; the few bits of grey also disguised by modern technology. Margie had let her own dark hair go completely grey – no point in fighting nature, she said – and had chosen an easy-to-manage short style. Typical Margie, thought Alison; she even looked good like that...

Life wasn't fair! Alison had inherited her father's figure – 'portly' according to his suit size, dumpy in her case. And if that wasn't bad enough, she shared his love of food, while Margie, tall and slim like their mother, was a health fiend who ate only when necessary.

Enough day-dreaming. Now she was alone to deal with all sorts of unimagined problems. Nothing – not even a lifetime of teaching – had prepared her for the present dilemma. Finding a smaller suitable home had been a nightmare, one she hoped would never be repeated.

On the brighter side, she'd mastered a subtle new language: estate-agent speak. Flat-hunting had taught her that 'within walking distance of the shops' meant 'a five-minute drive away'; 'compact' meant 'pokey'; 'needs a little TLC' was code for 'demolish and rebuild'; and, topping her hate list: 'at a realistic price' – realistic for Bill Gates or Donald Trump maybe!

After months of searching she'd found a small, sunny flat through a private sale. But now for the real agony. Fitting into the place. How had she managed to collect so much? Worse still, how could she be expected to get rid of most of her life's possessions? Mark's memorabilia had disappeared with him, but for her a lifetime of happy memories could not be so easily erased. Alison shook her head wearily. She'd anticipated a very different lifestyle when she retired from teaching. Cosy, quality time together, perhaps even a cruise...

She smiled ruefully at the aged black cat dozing blissfully on the couch. 'Don't worry, Joey, *I'll* never leave you. You'll soon get used to our new home – it's really feline-friendly. No need for me to put butter on your paws to stop you coming back here.' 'Would margarine have the same effect?' she wondered. 'Anyway you're far too fat and lazy to stray!'

Joey had arrived dramatically and unexpectedly. Alison had been driving on the freeway when a Gauteng car ahead of her had slowed down, and a small, black bundle had hurtled out of the window – and the car had sped off. Instinctively knowing that it was no ordinary parcel, she had stopped, picked up a terrified kitten and taken it straight home. Her daughter Gina had named the cat Jo – after her favourite character in *Little Women*. Gemma, her twin sister, had approved, because, she said, the cat was probably from Jo'burg. And so Jo, soon to be Joey, had entered their home, and their hearts. When Margie accused her sister of treating the cat as human, Alison justified herself: 'Some people talk to the trees; I talk to Joey! And she responds – sympathetically, not only critically!'

At least she's always here for me, smiled Alison at the apparently comatose cat.

She'd show Margie! Alison braced herself before walking into the study and almost tripping over the tottering towers of cassette tapes, CDs and old vinyl LP records piled on the carpet. She could anticipate her grandchildren's questions as they stared at the different sizes of vinyl records. Thank goodness they weren't visiting her today! She adored them, but right now she couldn't cope with their never-ending questions. For them the 'Why' stage had definitely not stopped at the age of three!

Alison made a half-hearted attempt at dusting the pile of records. 'You and I are an endangered species,' she said plaintively. 'In fact we're almost extinct!' She'd been advised by the owner of an 'antique' shop to recycle them into fruit bowls or handbags... 'Nice idea,' she had thought, 'but not for me.'

She flopped onto the floor and cautiously picked up the top

LP from the nearest pile. Strains of *The Blue Danube* floated past as she shrank back to childhood…a five-year old, dressed in her kindergarten 'rhythm tunic', pretending to sleep to the lilting melody which for some inexplicable reason was played at 'rest time'. Every so often she'd open an eye to see if her friends were really sleeping, or also just acting. 'Why must we sleep?' she'd ask herself, 'I want to dance!'

Alison defiantly grabbed the record cover and waltzed between the vinyl towers. For years she'd yearned to be in Vienna at New Year, waltzing at the Ball, but Mark had always refused to visit Austria in winter – and if she went now she'd have no one to dance with. Alison sighed in exasperation. 'I'd better just get on with this job…'

Sheepishly she removed Margie's list from the wastepaper basket, grabbed a purple koki pen and boldly labelled two of the leering cardboard boxes: 'In' and 'Out'. Later on she'd sort the Out pile into Give away/Throw Away/Sell, according to Margie's instructions. With a flourish she placed the *Famous Waltzes* LP in the Out carton. There, she had done something!

No need to be smug, hissed Joey, awakened by the plop of the record, *the LPs are scratched or warped; and in any case the record player is beyond repair. Not a generous gesture at all.*

The next record was *Popular Marches*. Alison's mind went back… Taller now, at senior school, filing into the hall for the daily assembly, to the persistent barking of the prefects: 'No talking!', 'Single file!' while the music teacher played stirring, patriotic tunes like 'Land of Hope and Glory'. She hummed the familiar tune and marvelled at how a song could transport one to another place, another age. The sixth-formers had seemed so grown up, yet when they had reached those heights themselves they hadn't felt confident and adult at all! Alison could hear the notes of the old school song, full of the Victorian spirit of adventure, of gaining courage and fighting fearlessly.

She could remember the words after all these years, but where had she left the koki? She'd read that tea was good for reviving the memory. Maybe she needed a break…

At school Alison's favourite activity had been 'sweet singing in the choir'. They would stand with hands demurely clasped in front, and genteel voices trilling classics such as 'Where'er You Walk' and 'Cherry Ripe'. The carefully enunciated consonants... 'Cool gales shall fan the glade...' remained indelibly in her mind. So different from the grandchildren who sang pop songs in up-to-the minute 'gear' and hairstyles – and then performed vibrant African songs, ululating and dancing enthusiastically, in traditional dress. Life was certainly becoming more interesting!

Their summer uniforms, unique in Pietermaritzburg, were dresses known as 'sprigs', probably because the pattern was sprigs of bluebells. Alison had never thought about the name before. We were the unquestioning generation, she thought to herself. Children were to be seen, not heard; to accept, not question. She could hear her grandchildren's astonished, 'But *why*, Gran?' Why indeed? No answer to that; it just 'wasn't done'.

The hems of the sprigs were a regulation two inches below the knee, the girls' hair was neatly brushed and, if long, was tied back with headbands known as snoods. Starched belts, for those who wanted to show off their waists. On their heads panama hats, usually dented from being sat upon, and frayed with age. She could still feel the hard strands pricking her head.

Short white socks, and stockings – before the miracle of pantyhose – for special occasions. Stockings, two singles per pack, that seemed to ladder as soon as you eased them on. Held up by dreadfully uncomfortable suspenders, the stockings gradually crept down in worm-like folds, with seams that moved from straight in the morning to zig-zag by lunchtime. 'Shoe-shined' brown buttoned or buckled shoes completed the picture. Those were the days before Velcro made life easy – Alison remembered struggling to sew on shoe buttons that were coming loose.

In winter we wore thick, brown 'bobby' socks – so unflattering, and the target of mocking comments from the neighbouring Merchiston schoolboys. No wonder we called them 'murky mud-rats'! The older College boys, sporting their straw bashers, knew better than to provoke us, even with those shapeless navy woollen berets perched on our heads.

School uniforms ruled the day, even after school hours. Full uniform was to be worn in public. You were even supposed to wear your hat to walk to your friend next door! And positively *no* eating in public in uniform. It too just 'wasn't done' – and you'd be in trouble if a prefect caught you.

Alison gazed at the record covers and the youthful faces of the pop stars of her teenage days. Some of them, surgically recycled, had returned to the stage for yet another decade of 'final' performances. Sadly, the magic had often disappeared – no Botox for an ageing voice.

On Saturday 'arvies' they'd gather – girls only! – around someone's ungainly radiogram, swooning or sulking, waiting to hear which pop star had made the coveted Number One spot on the Springbok Radio 'Hits of the Week'. The weekly build-up to this momentous event almost equalled the frenzy before the announcements of the winners of *Strictly Come Dancing* or *Idols*. Passionate comments about the looks – 'sex appeal' wasn't yet part of a nice girl's vocabulary – the morals and, almost as an afterthought, the singing of each one's heart-throb ruled the hour.

The pile of teenage records looked a little wobbly and dented, and Alison felt a bit that way herself. She closed her eyes and relived those days. Pat Boone or Elvis the Pelvis! 'April Love' versus 'Jailhouse Rock'! We could Rock Around the Clock in our Blue Suede Shoes or write Love Letters in the Sand!

And the fashions! The skirts-of-many-petticoats, which made their dresses look like open umbrellas, the broad elastic belts and flat 'kid glove' shoes – and their hair up in pony-tails. Just like in *Grease*!

How grown up they had felt when they progressed to shoes with stubby Cuban or Louis heels, and then to tottering in their first stiletto heels. Yes, those styles are back in fashion! 'Maybe I'll find some in my cupboard,' Alison grinned.

And the music of Victor Sylvester... She was back at the Saturday morning Dudley Andrews dancing class: slow, slow, quick-quick, the unmistakable smooth big band sound preparing us for the Saturday night parties and 'hops'. The quicksteps, and the waltzes (exhausting, despite their formality); the winding conga lines ('Come on; join in!'); the 'elimination' dances ('Anyone with fewer than three petticoats, please leave the floor'); the Tom Jones dances when you had to swop partners every time the music stopped, usually as soon as you were dancing with someone you fancied – though a welcome relief if you weren't! And the slow last dance, 'super' – as long as you had the right partner! Thanks to *Strictly Come Dancing*, the foxtrot, samba and cha-cha were in fashion again.

And of course the jiving, the wildly energetic bopping, and the rock 'n roll! The wonderful whirling and twirling, with ponytails flying and petticoats swinging – what *fun* it had been!

But life, they'd soon discovered, was not fair. No matter how many classes you attended, the hops were really fun only for the popular girls who twirled around the dance floor all evening, and close to torture for the rest – wallflowers, acne plastered over with pan stick, teeth encased in railway-tracks, and mouthing animated conversation with one's neighbours, while secretly watching the boys and praying 'Someone *please* ask me to dance; I can't go to the powder room again...'

Sometimes there was a breath-taking moment as the heart-throb of your dreams strode purposefully towards...the girl sitting next to you. Then, as you forced your facial muscles into a saccharine smile, wondering why you hadn't followed your instincts and stayed at home with a book, some pimply, greasy-haired drip shuffled towards you, crushing your hopes into despair... But at least you had progressed from the wall to the dance floor.

Alison came briefly back to reality. Those were *not* the days, my friend... She pulled out another record; it was Victor's turn for a spin. She twirled around the room: one, two, cha-cha-cha...

The Sixth Form Dance was the social highlight of the school year. The anticipation and post-mortems took priority over world disasters and low marks. Although the school didn't have its own matric dance, the girls were more than happy to accept invitations to other school dances. But even then they had to uphold the honour of the school by being 'appropriately' dressed: 'No backless dresses,' warned the headmistress – Miss Edwards, aka Eddie. 'And no canoodling in the cannas!' Not the kind of exhortation they'd expected from their staid headmistress!

How different it was now. Dresses were not mum's handiwork or the local dressmaker's. If only Eddie could see today's designer styles – and the prices! The event had become a spectacle almost on a par with the Oscar awards; there was even a national 'matric dress of the year' competition... Alison shook her head. And with liquor banned from school premises many school dances took place at sophisticated venues. Limos, top of the range 4×4s, even a helicopter to transport the young couples to the dance... How insensitive that was for the majority of the children – and, yes, they *were* children – and some of them couldn't go to their own school dances because their mothers were unable to pay the school fees... Alison shook her head again.

Her mind, seemingly of its own accord, wandered back to her past. No live bands or trendy clubs with flashing lights and mirror balls. We danced to records played on a wind-up gramophone or, if we were really lucky, a radiogram that could hold several records at once, so you didn't have to change them every few minutes. No e-pods or i-pods or any other kind of pods – nothing beyond the average granny's comprehension! *Our* dances stopped at midnight, and our fathers would drive us straight home, even if we were 'going steady'.

Alison smiled now, remembering the scandal when a group of boys had secretly set up a tape recorder in the powder room at their school dance! Several romances broke up after that bugging episode. She remembered postponing breaking up with her own boyfriend until after his school dance – she wasn't going to miss the social occasion of the school year! She'd never told Margie about that.

But times had changed; there were so many choices now. Girls danced alone, or in groups, or with other girls. It was hard to believe that the waltz was originally considered vulgar; no self-respecting mama would allow her daughter to be held so close by a young man – until Queen Victoria had given her stamp of approval! Alison glanced again at the discarded *Waltzes of Vienna* cover and grinned. Unlike the kindergarten children, the Victorians didn't sleep to the strains of Strauss waltzes!

She shook herself, in an attempt to bring herself properly back to the present and the work not exactly in progress. So many cartons, so little time… She would not stop until she'd got rid of the musical towers. No more reminiscing!

There, the LPs were finally dumped. Now for the little story-book records dating from the twins' young days. She stopped in mid-throw. No way! She'd never forget the cosy hours cuddled on the couch with Gina and Gemma eagerly waiting for Tinkerbell to play her glockenspiel tune, the signal to turn the page of the picture book. They'd loved those records, convinced that they were reading the story! Walt Disney and the fairy tales would stay!

And the cassettes? She hesitated – even though common sense reminded her that there was little point in hanging onto them since cassette players were 'out' and the music shops wouldn't fix them. Where could I play them? Alison brightened: They could be converted into CDs! But, no, she admitted, not by me! I'd never get round to it.

Accepting defeat, she returned the cassettes to the Out-box. 'Time to Say Goodbye,' she sang sadly, in not quite Sarah Brightman tones.

How she missed her friend Jen, who'd moved to Perth to be near her grandchildren. Jen, the epitome of order and discipline, knew exactly what she owned and where each item was kept. Everything had its place and that's where it stayed.

No frantic searching for urgent documents, papers all filed and accessible; diary meticulously filled in and regularly consulted. Each year Jen went through her cupboards, discarding whatever hadn't been used. If she were here, Alison thought to herself, there'd be no lingering or sentimental thoughts about what to discard. Life was simple: In/Out, what's the problem?

Talk about opposites! She missed their regular contact. Skype and email were wonderful, but nothing could replace a good chat and a cuppa! How often had she picked up the phone to share news or a joke before realising that Jen was no longer at the end of the local line? 'Pull yourself together!' she rebuked herself. 'There's work to be done!'

Well, she could be decisive about some things! Her classical CD collection was going with her, in its entirety. 'Finished and *klaar,*' as Dad used to say. Some things are non-negotiable!

Alison could trace her life through those CDs – something for her every mood, from the popular classics to jazz and opera. A new thought struck her. Had Mark taken his CDs with him to Sandton? If not, she might just keep them. They had similar tastes in music and had enjoyed going to concerts together. Now he'd have to endure Floozy's choice, the same music that their daughters enjoyed. Serve him right!

She envied Joey. What an uncomplicated life! A permanent carer to pack up the few necessities and drive you to your new home – all ready and waiting. Alison looked longingly at the kettle… 'Not a drop until the carpet is clear!' Echoes of disapproving Margie again…

No peeping to retrieve anything from the filled boxes. No looking back. Remember what happened to Lot's wife!

Several hours later Alison could see the pattern on the carpet. Happiness is a visible carpet, empty shelves, a sense of achievement – and an aching back!

Joey purred approvingly.

Alison filled the kettle and opened the biscuit tin. Reward! Time for some music; she removed a Beatles CD from the In-box. '*A Hard Day's Night…* I couldn't have said it better myself.'

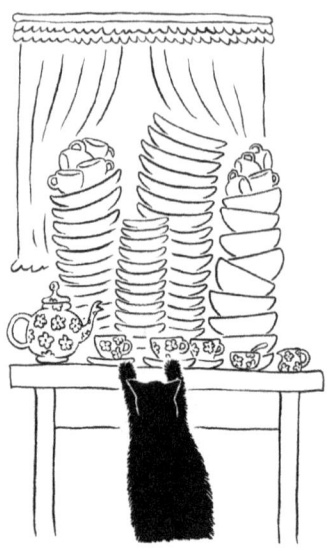

The Way We Were

'That's exactly what I'm doing at this very moment, Margie – sorting out the photos.' Alison hoped that she sounded convincing enough for her bossy sister. She really did intend tackling the photos that very day.

She replaced the receiver with unnecessary force and marched purposefully to the kitchen. Strong coffee with sugar, dark chocolate, good for the heart, especially in times of stress... A little early for vino? Her older sister in head prefect mode could literally drive her to drink!

While she was waiting for the kettle to boil, she stepped into the spare room to catch a glimpse of what lay ahead. Cautiously she opened the cupboard – and gaped at the photo-filled shoeboxes, chocolate boxes, plastic containers, and even a few albums and little brag-books, all lying higgledy-piggledy all the way to the top. Included in the crazy muddle were telegrams, letters and cards that marked the milestones of family life. Alison felt defeated before she'd begun. Perhaps just the childhood photos? She could leave the rest for Phase Two of the cupboard-clearing programme.

Ring ring… What did Margie want *now*?

But it was the welcome voice of Mandy, Alison's eldest grandchild: 'I'm doing a project on you, Gran! We have to find out all about growing up when you were young! It's for Miss Grainger; she always gives us such cool projects! I can't wait to get started! We've got to find out how different your childhood was from ours – school, home, games, friends, everything! Isn't that great, Gran? I know you've got loads of old photos in your cupboard! Can I come and look? And you can tell me everything!'

Now that was an incentive! Alison would do anything for her grandchildren, even go through the cupboard full of photos! Perhaps this was the sign that she needed, to push her into actually doing the tidying and decluttering of the photographs…

It might even be cathartic under the present circumstances… Working through the photographs with Mark in them would have to be done some time. Should she offer them to Mandy? He was her grandfather after all…

Mandy was right; she had plenty of material for her project. She'd put all the useful information into a Mandy-box – while she sorted out the photos and cards.

'Photos first. I'll start straight away! Then when I'm settled in the flat I'll learn how to load them onto CDs. So much easier for storing.' But that was followed by a voice in her head – a voice very like Margie's: 'You'll never destroy your celluloid memories.' Alison giggled wickedly. 'But that's okay; I'll end up with two sets, the originals and the backup copies!'

She stood on the shaky ladder heaving boxes from the cupboard. 'What a way to go,' she thought, melodramatically,

'Death by memories...' There were so many photos. Dad had seldom missed an opportunity to use his old concertina-like camera, 'Better than those new-fangled box ones,' he'd mutter proudly. What would he have said of taking photos from a cellphone!

She stared in desperation at the boxes on the floor. Why hadn't she systematically labelled and stuck them into albums like Margie always did? She must remind the girls to do that, though of course they probably didn't use albums anymore. Lucky IT generation!

This would take months. She'd sort the photos out at the flat.

But first, time for a CD while she decided what to tackle next. Music always helped in times of stress. Ah, the velvety voice of Nat King Cole – now that was music for relaxing. Alison always felt he was singing just to her... 'You're the cream in my coffee...' Coffee! She'd forgotten to make her coffee! How's that for synchronicity? It's a sign: stop everything; sit back and enjoy!

Extreme tension called for something to nibble with her coffee; she needed extra strength. In the fridge she found a chunk of ginger loaf in a plastic container, begging, 'Eat me!' That reminded her of the drawer of greying, well-used storage boxes, moulds, mixing bowls, cake-containers – all relics from the Tupperware party days – their lids, like socks in her washing machine, generally separated from their partners. Ouch! She knew what that felt like...

But first things first: Margie had recommended ginger and honey in boiling water as a health drink. Ginger in cake must also be acceptably healthy, Alison reassured herself.

Joey stood up, stretched languidly, and left the room, head and tail held high. *Pa-thetic!*

Alison carried the tray into the lounge, and settled down to enjoy 'a little repast' – that's what her former colleague, dear old Mr Arnold, would have called it. Determined to make the most of her self-imposed reprieve, she buttered the last slice while Nat King Cole wooed her melodiously.

Alison had strong feelings about the delicacies of occasion. Tea and coffee should be drunk in *cups*: mugs belonged to res rooms, 'digs' and her daughters' homes! 'Another one of Mum's eccentricities,' they'd nod to each other, as they added a cup and saucer to the tray of mugs. 'Part of the ageing process...' 'Age has nothing to do with liking good things,' she'd silently retort!

Alison had squandered – Margie's word – most of her first pay cheque on a dark green pottery tea set to celebrate her professional status. She treasured the remaining pieces. Was she another Hyacinth Bucket drooling over her hand-painted periwinkle blue floral set? She looked at her watch. It was almost time for a rerun of the programme – this decluttering business really showed how time goes by... She looked long-ingly at the television set then thought of the overflowing photo cupboard...and of Margie...

She glanced at the stinkwood cabinet, filled with her mother's 'best' tea set which hadn't been used for almost a century. Mum had judged it too delicate to use; Margie didn't like it – too impractical; Alison had never used it – too precious; and both Gemma and Gina had rejected it as 'not dishwasher safe'. 'How sad,' she sighed, 'too beautiful for this world!'

She'd start with the tea sets now! Anything to postpone the photograph-culling. Alison poured a second cup.

She'd become a coffee addict at varsity. When she was a child, tea had been enjoyed throughout the day, not only at prescribed 'tea times'. Florence, the family cook, would bring them their wake-up tray of steaming tea – in china cups. This need for regular 'fixes' had filtered down the generations. Oh those carefree pre-caffeine-fearing days! Nick and Glen, her sons-in-law, had bravely consumed numerous cups of tea until after announcing their engagements to her daughters, when both confessed to disliking the brew!

Alison sat back, enjoying every sip at the correct temperature. She hadn't always been so fussy. As a student she'd been too impatient to wait for the old-fashioned kettle to boil – any temperature would do! But her flatmate Sophie, a music student with perfect pitch, would shout from her room, 'Not yet! It hasn't reached F sharp!'

One memory stimulated another. Res life had encouraged creativity. They discovered that one could successfully boil eggs in a kettle – they seldom cracked, despite bouncing on the element – and that a toothbrush handle could double as a knife to slice her Aunt Ann's delicious cakes. Who could wait until the next meal to borrow one from the dining hall?

Food (glorious food!) had been extremely important to Alison as a student – and when she became a teacher. Even now, she admitted to herself. But why not? She'd even categorised her teaching posts according to the quality and quantity of the refreshments provided at Break. The elite Cape Town school at which she'd taught music to 'young ladies' had come out top!

At that time, Alison was living in rather dismal digs: a sparsely furnished room in a musty old house owned by a Miss Havisham look-alike. As in the Dickensian home, little appeared to have been moved or cleaned for years. Lena, the bandy-legged, arthritic domestic 'help', would do a cursory flap past the furniture with a threadbare duster, then disappear into her room to listen to radio serials, emerging only when Miss Havisham's bell imperiously summoned her to open the 'medicinal' bottle of gin. Just like *Madam & Eve*'s Granny Anderson!

That accommodation had definitely been 'lodging without board'. The kitchen was a real health hazard, and in any case Alison never had time for breakfast before the frantic early morning dash to the bus stop. Wearing a thick coat over several layers of warm clothing, scarf and plastic over-shoes, she would alight from the bus and trudge up the hill, with her umbrella performing acrobatics in the south-easter and the rain viciously slapping her face. Staggering along in the early-morning darkness, propelled by the crazy umbrella in one hand and the obligatory teacher's basket in the other, she felt like a cartoonist's dream. Chauffeur-driven luxury cars, with her smug-looking pupils sitting regally in the back, splattered muddy water onto her already-drenched clothes. None of them ever stopped to offer her a lift.

No wonder Small Break and Big Break were the highlights of Alison's day! Elegant silver teapots and thin china cups and saucers, with doily-lined platters of ridiculously dainty sandwiches to be savoured as delicately and as slowly as possible! One tried not to appear greedy, however ravenous one was feeling. It seemed to Alison that every time she took a bite Miss McLoughlin, the lady principal, would ask her a question: 'Have your theory books arrived yet, Miss Gordon?' In time Alison had mastered the art of chewing, swallowing and chatting without choking. 'Multi-tasking' it would be called in today's jargon.

The first note of the end-of-break bell was the cue for the perpetually disapproving vice-principal – 'Mrs Grumpy' to the younger staff – to take up her position at the staffroom door. Her frown-furrowed forehead rose in condemnation, her tight sausage-rolled 'permanent waves' trembling as she shooshed us out of the door, declaring grimly with meaningful pauses between each word 'I think that was the bell!' Not the ideal moment for another sandwichette!

Those problems dwindled to nothing when Alison changed jobs. 'Tea' at her new school was a culture shock. Not only did the teachers have to pay each month for stewed, aluminium-flavoured tea, but they were restricted to one cup each. On her first day there Alison had silenced the noisy staffroom chatter by automatically refilling her cup. Her mum, also a teacher, had always said: 'The first cup is to relieve your throat; the second to enjoy.' This school's Mrs Grumpy – every school has one, Alison soon realised – announced self-righteously, with her head slightly cocked to one side: 'We all pay each month for *one* cup of tea or coffee at each break. If you *need* a second cup you must *pay* accordingly.'

No daily 'little somethings' here either. For formal occasions there were doughy cakes, covered in thin, sickly-coloured icing from the school kitchen; the teachers provided packets of assorted biscuits on their birthdays.

Alison returned home after she and Mark became engaged. There she was happy to accept a temporary job at a local high school, filling in for a music teacher who was on sick leave. In this staffroom she discovered that some professional categories were 'more equal than others'. The lowest order of the ladder was the temporary, newly qualified teacher, and, teetering on the very bottom rung, the temporary, newly qualified *music* teacher. 'Not a real subject, mere entertainment,' the Head of Science had remarked dismissively in Alison's presence.

On her first day there, balancing a thick, crested cup and saucer in her hand, Alison meandered around numerous tables and chairs in the staffroom until she found a vacant chair. She was totally ignored by all until the new Grumpy – a cantankerous replica of Queen Mary – informed her, in words eloquently tinged with steel, 'This is *my* chair. When you have taught here for as long as I have, then you may sit at this table.' Alison was stunned. How very welcoming, she thought, and removed herself from the staffroom for the rest of her stay.

She created her own break-time routine. At the beginning of the month – while she could still afford it – she'd walk to the nearest tearoom to enjoy a solitary cuppa and a sandwich. (When she told them this story, her grandchildren had been fascinated by the word 'tearoom' and had asked her whether coffee was also served there!) As the month progressed and finances diminished she'd swallow her hurriedly home-thrown-together sandwiches and gulp down a plastic cup of tea-in-the-flask in the cloistered environment of her music-cell. Alison shuddered as she remembered how cold that little room had been in winter.

Fortunately her pupils were more welcoming and she thoroughly enjoyed teaching them. However, the permanent teacher soon recovered, the staffroom chairs were safe from intruders and Alison was unemployed once more.

But the saga was not over. Her salary! Despite having arrived within an hour of receiving the call to help out at the school, she'd had to wait months before being paid. Apparently her qualifications, acceptable enough for teaching, needed a more thorough investigation before she could be paid. When she went to the Education Department offices to collect the long-awaited cheque, surprise, surprise, the offices and corridors of the finance floor were completely vacant. They were all at tea!

After several jobless months – fortunately she was staying at home with her parents – Alison was offered a locum at the prestigious boys' high school.

On her first day she caught the bus, and, as it approached the school, she pressed the buzzer.

'No, dear,' called the concerned driver, 'this is the boys' school. The girls' school is the next stop.' As if she didn't know – this was her home town! Alison smiled, waved and stepped off the bus.

As she walked up the long, winding driveway she noticed the boys nudging each other and staring at her with quizzical expressions. Were her stocking seams crooked or was her petticoat hanging out? Quite unperturbed, with the confidence of youth, a teaching diploma and a job, even if only a locum, she asked one of the boys for directions to the staffroom.

Complete silence greeted her entrance. A dozen or so men froze and stared, wide-eyed, as if in the presence of an alien. Late-comers stopped in their tracks with similar stunned expressions. She realised almost immediately that one of the teachers was standing outside the door warning: 'Watch it! There's a female in there!' To which the general response, 'Don't be ridiculous!' blended into a stammered 'Good morning...'

She was the only female teacher in the school. By tea time she'd received a note from the headmaster instructing her to spend breaks with the lady secretary in her office. 'He thinks they can't control their language for twenty minutes!' she explained. 'But they're *teachers* – what other antiquated ideas are they passing on to the pupils?' Alison asked in astonishment.

For her it was a lost opportunity: she'd hoped to meet some congenial 'talent'. No chance of becoming the femme fatale of the staffroom. 'And I never even found out if there was another Omar Sharif in that male haven...' Alison sighed.

Her moment of revenge had come when the headmaster offered her a permanent post. Although she enjoyed teaching the boys and had made friends with some of her colleagues outside the staffroom, it was with some pleasure that she declined the offer. She had accepted a permanent post at a school in Durban where, as it turned out, her presence was not extraordinary.

Gemma and Gina, growing up in a more gender-friendly era, had made her retell the story ad nauseam.

Alison suddenly noticed the time on the mantelpiece clock: 'I've been on a nostalgia trip for a whole hour!' she gasped.

The clock was a hideous owl-shaped insult to both birds and clockmakers. The eyes, which marked the hours and minutes, gave the owl a constantly drunken gaze. It had been a wedding gift from a friend of Mark's with a bizarre sense of humour. Why had they not got rid of it decades ago, she wondered. Maybe she'd send it to Mark.

Let the decluttering begin! Never mind Mark; she heaved the owl into the Out-box. There must be someone, somewhere who'd love it! She looked around for more victims. Those awful ashtrays advertising various brands of whisky? Away with them!

Positive action made her feel reckless and liberated. She grabbed two ghastly vases taking up space in the display cabinet – Aunt Becky's gifts to Mum, who would never admit that they were tasteless and downright ugly. Out! She wrapped the unwanted articles hastily in old newspaper – no point in letting them get damaged. Why had she never had the courage to do this before?

While still in the mood she made a quick decision about her mum's crystal vases. She'd keep one and give the other to Mum's friend Molly, who'd always admired them. On second thoughts, Molly might like both of them! Definitely not dishwasher-safe for the younger generation.

I'll phone Margie with the good news! This is fun!

Ignoring the cupboard of photographs, she glanced instead at the silver tea set on a tray engraved with a message of wedding congratulations to her parents. A family heirloom? She'd have no room for it, the girls didn't want it ('Who has time to clean silver, Mum?') and who would buy an engraved gift? Perhaps the inscription could be removed? She'd ask Margie! In any case, as the elder daughter, it was Margie's duty to keep the antique. Then Alison remembered that her sister already had a similar one. She'd keep it. Her grandchildren would bless her, and in the meantime she could use the jug and teapot as vases, pretty and original...

Joey rolled her almond-shaped green eyes: *Nice try*.

And the hand-painted, unused bone china tea set? Alison loved its delicate beauty, but, again, no family takers. 'No way! You're the only one who uses cups and saucers, Mum!' She washed and dried each piece with care, admired them for the last time and placed them, wrapped carefully this time, in a separate carton for her antique dealer friend to sell... She felt quite altruistic...maybe it was time for someone else to enjoy and perhaps even use it. Then again, why couldn't she keep it? She could hear her ultra-organised friend Jen: 'Keep Only What's Useful.' Alison looked around furtively. There was no one to stop her. Into the In-box!

A satisfactory day's work! Even though she hadn't tackled the photographs, she'd made some important decisions, got rid of a few unnecessary possessions and kept some family treasures for the next generation.

The next move was obvious. 'Spoil yourself. You deserve it,' she smugly mimicked the television advertisement as she filled the kettle... Now where was that healthy dark chocolate?

Food, Glorious Food

Four o'clock! Alison sat up in bed with a sense of foreboding after another sleepless night.

'It's all too much,' she wailed. 'We Taureans hate change.' She wasn't good at making decisions. She'd had no choice in accepting a new single way of life, and a new home, but choosing what to take and what to leave was proving really painful.

'I need the house police!' She was the perfect candidate for the television house-cleaning series! She pictured the entire scenario in Hi Definition. The team would rush in, kisses all round, shriek and flap their hands enthusiastically, and set their chaos-removal machine on 'Go'. In a twinkle they'd remove the clutter and place her remaining necessities in Jen-like order in the transformed flat, now a minimalist's delight – while she luxuriated in a boutique hotel!

After a complete make-over, Alison, who now resembled Angelina Jolie, would be sipping cocktails at the hotel pool with Richard Gere and George Clooney vying for her attention, until – tra la – a chauffeured limo would drive her to view first her empty, spotless old house, and then on to the sparkling new flat. Artistically arranged furniture, neatly stacked cupboards, walls glowing with collages of her photos...

She'd read that positive thinking could achieve miracles, so why not dream?

She often wondered how the recipients of television home make-overs honestly felt about their new-look homes. She'd heard one unhappy lady yell to the horrified team: 'It's *horrible!* I think I'm going to be sick!' As far as I'm concerned, Alison said to herself, they can have carte blanche. Just relieve me of any decisions! Any style; any colour – well, within reason... Just *do it*, please!' No more 'I'm busy spring-cleaning' excuses when friends popped in unexpectedly. She'd seen a comforting sign on someone's desk: 'A messy office is a sign of a genius.' 'Ha! That's me!' she laughed.

Joey shifted on the bed. *Who are you kidding?*

Back to reality! She'd dreamed her impossible dream. It was time for a pick-me-up cuppa.

Joey languidly opened an eye in apparent agreement. *One milk, no tea.*

Once she'd put the kettle on, Alison took another look at Margie's Commandments. *Spend twenty minutes clearing the first mess in sight.* Not a problem, she thought ruefully, looking around. *Then treat yourself to a reward.* Now we're talking! Very un-Margie-like – she'd have cleared the entire house in one dynamic session! Not that Margie had any clutter in her perfectly organised home. But she certainly knew her younger sister!

'The first mess in sight.' No need to look far! The coffee table. Twenty minutes: she set the kitchen timer. Ready! Steady! Go! She briskly removed the telephone directory, her diary (*That's* where it had got to!), two pens, one without its innards, her cellphone hidden under yesterday's newspaper – stopping briefly to check and reply to several missed calls and SMSes and to skim-read the Hatched/Matched/Dispatched columns – her current library book, horribly overdue, and a roll of sticky tape that had at some point become inextricably attached to a stray teaspoon, a pair of scissors and the one remaining babushka of a set of six that her youngest grandchild hadn't yet managed to destroy.

Alison threw the articles into a paper bag – recycled, Margie! – to be sorted out later. One thing at a time…

Tring! Time's up! 'One uncluttered table! Well done, Alison!' Margie's 'work and reward' system might be child-appropriate, but it worked for her! Signs of her second childhood?

Exhilarated with success, Alison grabbed a duster and the spray polish and attacked the coffee table until it glowed! Look at the grain of the wood! What a lovely piece of furniture! To think that she had intended throwing it out! Certainly not now!

Joey's gentle purring deepened into a groan.

One small step for decluttering, one large step for Alison. Thank you, Margie!

What next? She was on a roll! She ignored the rickety old wooden bookcase on which layers of books were precariously scattered, as if they'd been overtaken by a minor tsunami. She could sniff out a book sale, wherever it might be: at a flea-market, in the foyer of a mall or, best of all, at her favourite bookshop, where she could relax with a bargain and the best coffee in town. She used the library regularly, but there were some books she just had to own. But how had she allowed her collection to get in such chaos? And her beloved paperback novels, many in a state of dishevelment, were crying out for attention. She'd repair them as soon as she'd disentangled the sticky tape…

Her old friends Di and Pam, concerned that Alison was becoming anti-social after the divorce, had bullied her into joining their book club – but their reading tastes were so different. They devoured gruesome murder stories, lapping up every gory detail. In Alison's opinion the daily newspapers provided more than enough violence and horror. 'Give me Morse 'midst the spires of Oxford, and, for a dash of Italian spice, Brunetti in Venice!' After months of always being in a minority of one in the choice of books, she regretfully resigned from the club. What she did miss though was the friendly chatter, the laughter – and the delicious teas!

Food again! Idea! She'd begin with her recipe book collection! 'A very good place to start,' she sang. When she and Mark got married Alison had overcome her ignorance of cooking; she was now addicted to the television cooking channel, unable to resist buying celebrity recipe books – or, for that matter, any cookery book! From baking to braai-ing, from pasta to *potjie*, she read them like novels, ticking recipes for future use, then abandoning them for the safe trusted ones. A harmless pleasure, surely? A food-lovers book club? Now there's a novel idea!

'But you *must* have studied domestic science at school?' Aunt Becky was incredulous. 'I thought you'd gone to a *good* school!' Her favourite nephew's fiancée was domestically challenged! In an earlier era she might have collapsed onto a chaise longue and inhaled smelling salts.

Mark's indomitable aunt had immediately sent Alison a large, hard-covered brown volume: *Domestic Instruction for the New Bride*. 'Bor-ing!' – to borrow the grandchildren's over-used term.

'Take great care of this and study it carefully,' she'd threatened. 'Even I found it invaluable.' Enticing topics included cleaning floors; washing, by hand, and ironing; home-made remedies for childhood ailments and eradicating cockroaches and other household pests. 'And human pests?' thought Alison irreverently. Some of the advice was unintentionally hilarious.

'In order to be attractive *at all times* the young bride should get up early to cleanse and make up her face and brush her hair, one hundred times, before her husband awoke.' It wouldn't do to be seen in a dishevelled early-morning state!

'What about *his* early-morning state?' she thought. 'And before he returns from work to enjoy her delicious home-cooked meal,' – Alison giggled – 'the young bride must have his newspaper, slippers, a drink and snack ready for him!' Best of all, read Alison on the verge of hysteria, 'she should not enquire about her husband's day at the office or pester him with domestic trivia until he indicates his readiness for such conversation'! So not twenty-first century!

Why then, was it still on the bookshelf? Fear of Aunt B, she admitted. It must be Africana by now! Off to a library or historical museum! She rejected the malicious thought of sending it to Floozy, and dropped the outdated and offensive tome into the Out-box.

Culinary skills before marriage? Both Alison and Kathy, her flat-mate at the time, had enjoyed a carefree life, unshackled by such mundane thoughts! Study a recipe after a long day's teaching? You must be joking! They occasionally splurged on takeaway dinners bought on the way home from school, or created meals, tactfully described as 'interesting' by friends, with the aid of a tin-opener. The sight of the familiar Chicken-Out container from the nearby take-away restaurant brought relief to their guests. Edible chicken curry, not another dicey gastronomic experiment. Kathy's ungrateful brother, Gerald, had once commented that their Sea Point flat was 'fortunately close to the Medical Centre'.

Welcome relief had come from Kathy's mother who would send food parcels from Bloemfontein with anyone careless enough to mention that they were visiting Cape Town. Knowing how clueless they both were, she'd label every home-made meal: 'Peri-peri chicken. Heat in oven at 360° (Fahrenheit in those days) or eat cold. Keep in fridge'; 'Biscuits. Close tin properly'. Oh, for one of those date biscuits now…

They'd had no recipe books, but instructions on every kind of diet filled the flat. They'd tried them all! The *All-protein*, the *All-carbohydrate*, the *Eggs-only* (they soon became 'eggsperts' – Gerald's word – boiled, fried, scrambled, omelettes, they'd learnt quickly!), the *Apples-only*, even the *Liquid Detox* diet (that one had dire results!). The *Weigh-Every-Crumb* diet was the shortest-lived of all. Accurately weigh food? It took all the pleasure out of eating! The diet they'd kept to most easily was a 'fat only' diet. A food-lover's paradise; everything had to be fried! Their Sunday Breakfast Special: fried brinjals, fried tomatoes, fried mushrooms, fried eggs, all served on bread fried in the same pan. Yet, to their disappointment, no matter how often and at what hour of the day or night they stood on the bathroom scale, their weight kept escalating! Luckily we didn't know about cholesterol, Alison grinned.

Joey stirred again. *What's cholesterol?*

Alison's kitchen tea had been the usual girly event, side-splitting for her friends, a nightmare for her. Gerald had let the secret out, leaving Alison to pretend surprise and joy while inwardly cursing Kathy who had reneged on her promise of no kitchen tea. After the ordeal she'd gazed curiously at the kitchen gadgets and domestic necessities. What was she supposed to do with them? Produce interesting, tasty meals *every day?*

Mark's place was definitely not in the kitchen. He'd lived at home until their marriage. His mother cooked his favourite meals, rarely allowed him to wash up afterwards, never mind actually cooking something. Gina and Gemma, perhaps made wise by their mother's experience, had cleverly both married men who enjoyed cooking.

Cousin Zoë, a domestic executive of several years, was blunt. 'You can read? You can cook!' and presented her with *Perfect Meals in Minutes!* The cover showed a slim Mrs Perfect, flashing a Macleaned smile and with gleaming Sunsilked hair immaculately flicked up. Her tiny waist proved that she didn't taste a morsel of the effortless gourmet dinners she prepared in her spotless shiny kitchen! *She* would have been a worthy niece for Aunt Becky! Despite hating Mrs Perfect at first sight, Alison blessed Zoë for the book. User-friendly recipes with illustrations for the raw cook. No matter how many others she'd bought since – just look at the bookshelf – Mrs P's recipes were her fool-proof favourites! Battered, tattered and splattered from constant use, it had pride of place in the In-box!

Next, a bulging folder choc-a-block with tempting but untried recipes torn from magazines and newspapers. Who was she fooling? To her shame even now, in the midst of packing, she'd been adding tempting recipes, kidding herself that one day she'd try them. Another addiction.

Joey shook her head.

Alison found herself empathising with the BBC television dance competition judges – or 'djoodges' – whose job was to decide 'who will stay and who will go'. Some of the recipes were brown with age. She took a deep breath and forced herself not to read the cut-out recipes again, just in case. '*Out!*' she shouted bravely, still clutching the folder.

Joey opened an eye; this was getting interesting.

With a smile of satisfaction, Alison added the folder to the Out-box. *By Jove, she's done it!* Joey was impressed.

Progress! Time to celebrate! Coffee! Irish?

Gimme the cream, purred Joey.

The percolator, used only for celebrations, gurgled gleefully. She poured the rich, aromatic liquid into a cup, added a drop of cold milk and more than a little sugar, and after a brief hesitation opened a packet of shortbread. The feeling of doom was definitely lifting.

But not for long. Sudden panic: what was the date? She grabbed the laminated calendar from the bookshelf and whistled with relief. The girls' birthday was *next* week! It wasn't that she was forgetful (heaven forbid!), but decluttering seemed to have taken over her life. The weeks raced by so fast that every day seemed to be Friday! She blessed her daughters for their thoughtful Mother's Day gift, a calendar with photos of each family member digitally printed on the appropriate birthday date. No excuses now!

Would she ever forget their first birthday! Gina and Gemma, the only twins in the family were a source of interest and fascination. The low-key afternoon tea for the immediate family had escalated to include the 'sisters and the cousins and the aunts', twelve in all. Thank goodness for her tea set for twelve. True to form, the little girls overslept. Despite her mother's advice, she'd woken them, and the little cherubs that she'd hoped to show off turned into grouchy monsters! She'd dressed them in the identical pink frilly dresses Aunt Becky had given them – brownie points, surely? – and prayed that they wouldn't be sick all over the bows and lace before Aunty B arrived to inspect her great-nieces.

After settling the girls in their highchairs Alison carried the overloaded tea tray towards the dining room. As she walked through the hall, the doorbell trilled and, as if on cue, both girls started crying. In a fluster now, she balanced the tray on one knee and opened the door. The tray slid to the floor with a crash of splintering china; the girls' screams crescendoed to a frenetic fortissimo, and Aunt Becky boomed, 'Coo-ee! We're here!'

Alison gathered up the shards of the shattered tea set and deposited them in the dustbin. The Mad Hatter's Tea Party was alive and well!

'I'm famished!' announced Aunty B, pinching the babies' tear-flooded cheeks and ignoring the domestic drama. 'And thirsty!' added Aunt Lily, always two steps and an echo behind her domineering elder sister. Alison's mother began chatting gently about nothing in particular; the crying eventually stopped and all waited expectantly for the party to begin.

In the kitchen Alison gazed helplessly at the remaining four cups and eleven saucers. If only her guests had all been cats – Cheshire cats? – they could have lapped their tea from the saucers. What *was* she to do?

Restraining herself from leaving the party and going to bed, as her flatmate Kathy had done under extreme stress one evening, Alison poured tea for the four most revered (read 'oldest') of the guests. Minutes later she whipped their still warm and not all quite empty cups off to the kitchen where she hurriedly washed and filled them for the next relay. Thank goodness for Mum, who chatted non-stop in an attempt to restore sanity.

Mark, held up at work, arrived in time to help blow out the candles. The birthday cake, iced by Alison with more enthusiasm than expertise, was surprisingly light. 'An improvement on your last effort,' was Aunt Becky's graceless praise. As if in reply Gemma threw her plastic cup of juice in the air, splashing orange juice all around her. The children's wailing chorus started up once more. Gran grabbed both girls, announced that it was bath time for the drenched, cake-covered one-year olds and shooed the guests out.

'I could have done with another cup of tea!' declared Aunt Becky imperiously.

'Tea – and birthday cake,' echoed Aunt Lily, dormouse-like.

'And she never even *cut* the cheesecake; I was looking forward to that.' Aunt Becky was indignant.

'Forget the tea,' Alison whispered to Mark. 'Give me something stronger. Now!' For once Alison was happy to abandon the past and return to her decluttering.

She found a photo album filled with exotic recipes from various cooking demonstrations. On Saturday nights their group of newly married friends would meet to sample each other's versions of the expert's dishes, some more memorable than others. Most unforgettable had been Di's Italian pasta disaster when the Frascati flowed too freely and the Neapolitan songs drowned the oven timer's tinkling so that pasta and pot united as one burnt offering.

Their next craze was floral art! Armed with flowers and greenery they'd rushed to flower arranging courses then tried to replicate the various shapes and styles for their Saturday night dinner parties. Short and tall, triangles, rectangles, flowers flowing from one candlestick to another, Alison had tried them all. Sadly, her skills in this area were minimal. Barbara, their teacher, would gaze at her efforts and shake her head sorrowfully. 'Hmmm, not quite, dear; let me help,' and instantly turn them into works of art. Fortunately the natural look soon came into fashion and Alison could present a fairly acceptable arrangement by just dumping a bunch into a vase!

How much effort had gone into those evenings! Thank goodness fancy dinner parties were out!

'And so are you!' she said, grabbing the floral art file and adding it to the rapidly filling Out-box.

Alison was learning to enjoy Mark-free socialising. The simple spontaneity of bring and share, quiche and coffee, 'whatever's in your fridge'. How food fashions had changed.

So had the conversation, at least to some extent! On children: same topics, different generation. The interminable discussions of their own children's development (not potty-trained yet?), their cute sayings (do you know what Michael asked me?), their progress at nursery schools (she can tie a bow already), the pros and cons of various schools (have you seen their matric results?) were replicated in discussions of their grandchildren. It's only the names that change: just replace 'Michael' with 'Zach' and you wouldn't know the difference.

Their personal topics had changed though; they now revolved around their ailments – arthritis, blood pressure, diabetes – with remedies ranging from granny's home remedies to those hot off the internet. Cataract procedures ('I'd forgotten the world was so colourful'), hip and knee replacements ('When are you having the other one done?'), coronary bypasses ('Oh, you only had *three*?'). So much to look forward to!

And the health problems affected more than one's own body. Choosing a menu these days involved far more than seasonal products. Food intolerance, allergies, illnesses and eccentricities... Eliminate fish, meat, sugar, dairy, avocados, sesame seeds, strawberries and kiwi fruit – no matter what you wanted to cook, there'd be someone who couldn't eat it. Alison herself was guilty of some food quirks. She just couldn't eat fish that looked like a fish – even the innocuous herring had to be tailed and decapitated before she would eat it.

Fish in any form for me, dreamed Joey.

Their dinner service – a wedding gift from Aunt Becky – had each plate realistically painted with a different species of fish, each in all its glazed-eyed glory. Margie, who had no such qualms readily swopped it for her innocuous white set! Just as well they had different tastes!

Joey looked at her for a long time, seemed to sigh, then went back to sleep! *Enough is enough!*

The phone disturbed her thoughts. Margie! 'I'm doing well – getting rid of some recipe books!'

'I suppose it's a start,' Margie commented, instantly dampening Alison's enthusiasm. 'But you must be ruthless, Ally. I suppose you still have books that use the old measurements! It's half a century since we changed to metric! Get with it!' Alison had originally doubted that she'd ever master the metric system, but now pounds and ounces were a mystery! But she still had those books... No mention to Margie that she'd just bought a new book – mouth-watering Mediterranean recipes with water-colour sketches and fascinating stories of their places of origin. Well, it was on a sale...

She made a pile of the antiquated recipe books, successfully stifling the urge to re-read them. 'Dust-collectors! Out you go!'

Alison felt more than virtuous. Lunch time!

Joey agreed.

Yesterday

Alison lay in bed. So much to do, so much to think about. She resented the fact that Mark had had it so easy. He'd made the decision to end their marriage and had a brand new life waiting for him. No pressure. She'd been left with the really tough decisions.

Just as well they had agreed on the fate of the furniture. She'd take with her whatever she wanted, as long as it could fit into the flat. The rest would go to an auction sale.

He'd taken most of his things when he left, but there were some things neither of them had thought about. The tools were definitely Mark's department – she'd need a handyman now, with his own set of tools. She had to admit that Mark could fix anything – except his marriage – and was justifiably proud of his ability. She'd put the tools into a new box, labelled M.

What else needed to go into that box? She'd forgotten the huge envelope with their certificates and diplomas. Alison had never had hers framed and Mark had framed only his most prestigious one for the office. When the girls were at school, Mark had encouraged her to do a teaching course at the local training college – so that she could teach more than just music. She'd enjoyed being a mature student, though rushing off to organise birthday parties during exams had been a slight problem, but Mark had been quite helpful. It was at training college that she and Di had become so friendly.

Where was that envelope? Probably in one of the drawers at the bottom of Mark's wardrobe... In that wardrobe there was also his mother's silver cutlery set. She'd left it to both of them – and Mark hadn't taken it. But would Gina or Gemma want it? Alison was tired of her daughters' excuses about valuable things needing too much time and care. She'd keep it for Mandy! Mark's mother had been besotted with her granddaughter and would have liked her to have it. Then Gemma would *have* to take it! That was a quick and clever solution!

Despite her shock and sadness at dividing up what had been their life together, Alison had been delighted to give Mark his favourite picture, that awful Spanish lady leering from behind her fan. When he brought it home, years before, she'd hung it in an inconspicuous place behind the study door, hoping no one would think it was her taste. Now Floozy could enjoy it! Alison could imagine her taste in paintings...

Alison stretched, but she wasn't ready to get up yet (nor was Joey). She looked at the pale rectangle on the bedroom wall where their wedding photograph had hung. 'My glamorous bride,' he'd called her, misty-eyed on their wedding day. Their wedding song: 'I Only Have Eyes for You'... Oh yeah? Maybe he had cataracts. What would Floozy choose? 'Love is Lovelier the Second Time Around'?

Theirs had been a lovely wedding: 'Even Aunt Becky said so,' her mum had boasted proudly – though Aunt Becky couldn't resist adding that her own daughter Elspeth's wedding had been 'an evening affair, with a live band'. Alison and Mark's reception had been at the Imperial, Maritzburg's most gracious hotel, with a friend playing the electric organ. But look at the photos: both sets of parents beaming with joy. The wedding cake, made by their next-door neighbour, had been admired by all. Alison, who disliked marzipan, hadn't wanted a wedding cake, but Aunt Becky was determined that you couldn't have a wedding without one and Alison had succumbed to her nagging pressure. Decades later when Gina had insisted on delicately iced cupcakes instead of a wedding cake, Alison hadn't objected. The cake might 'make' a wedding, but not a marriage that lasts; Alison sighed.

Family and friends had made an effort to be there, some colleagues even driving through the night from Cape Town. Alison remembered how a black cat had walked in front of the bridal car driven by Mark's dad. At the time she'd thought it was a lucky sign...

She shook her head. Floozy would have been singing nursery rhymes at the time of their wedding... When she married Mark would they invite the grandchildren, or even worse, Gina and Gemma, to be in their wedding retinue? Would they accept?

'Turn off the bitter button,' she cautioned herself. 'If I carry on like this people will start saying "One can't blame him; she's such a misery".'

It was all so out of character. Mark was so proud of his girls – he didn't stop smiling for a month after their birth! A hands-on father, bathing them at weekends, to the annoyance of the other young fathers in their block of flats. They teased him for spoiling the market!

He'd loved taking them for walks along the beachfront when they were babies, patiently answering the questions of the passers-by: Were they twins? Were they both girls? Such silly questions when they were dressed in identical pink babygrows and those hideous bonnets that Alison's mum had insisted they wear!

He'd bought a Cine 8 machine and became obsessed with recording every moment of their lives, milestone or not. Almost every birthday party, though fortunately not the first disastrous one, and certainly not their birth, as is common today.

Their favourite game as toddlers had been hiding behind the curtains – with their feet sticking out! – and calling: 'Here we are, Daddy,' in case he couldn't find them! He'd been a wonderful father. How could he behave so badly now?

Her reverie was interrupted by the ring of the telephone. Surely not Margie? Relief; it was Pam. 'I just called to find out how you're doing. I'm working from home today if you need me.' Pam was the friend who most understood how difficult it was for Alison to cope with her situation.

Joey snuggled up to her on the bed. Alison looked at her watch. She'd better get up and do something!

'Don't tempt me, Joey,' she said, 'I'd like to spend the day in bed too, but I can't. Come on, let's have breakfast.'

As she buttered her toast Alison's mind went back to her biggest problem – leaving the house where she'd lived for so many years. She really loved it. Such happy memories – until Mark's bombshell.

She remembered how hard it had been, finding their first (and only!) house. She wouldn't even get out of the car to look at a house if it had a swimming pool. With two toddlers under two? But she'd fallen in love with their present house before realising that there was a swimming pool at the back. No problem – she'd turn it into a rose garden!

The pool firm had dismissed her suggestion with disdain, and Mark had persuaded her that he'd take care of the pool fencing and security – which he did, making the stakes closer together than municipal regulations, and with a lock that clanged throughout the neighbourhood when it opened or closed. So she'd eventually agreed to keeping the pool. Even so, she used to have nightmares about the twins standing on boxes to climb over the fence, and even when they were at high school she wouldn't allow them to swim without an adult to watch them. Not that she'd have been any good in an emergency, but she could at least phone for help if needed. Fortunately her services were never needed.

Mark had taught the girls to swim using Bentley belts. They seldom tired of playing ring a ring o' roses in the pool with him, laughing when he changed the words to 'all fall up' as he lifted them out of the water. She could still hear the delighted screams of 'More, Daddy, more!' Would he have the same energy with his new family? Floozy would surely want her own children... Well. Charlie Chaplin had produced children when he was in his seventies. She smiled ruefully. She knew how exhausting it was just baby-sitting at her age. And at least grandchildren went home at night! Mark adored and spoilt his grandchildren; how would he explain the arrival of a new family to them? They would be older than their uncle or aunt! Alison shook her head; she felt almost sorry for Mark.

She looked out of the window at the garden, full of flowering shrubs. The gardening tools? The new owners wanted the garden furniture, so why not let them have the lawn mower and garden tools as well? Brilliant! But it would take time for her to be able to walk past the garden section at the supermarket, and she'd miss choosing plants at the nursery – she and her friends would just have to go straight to the coffee shop! But on the other hand she'd enjoy turning her own little patio into a pretty and useful mini-garden.

What next? She remembered the old suitcase at the top of Mark's wardrobe. She'd fill it with whatever else he'd left behind. She reached up and yanked it down – and nearly toppled over under its weight. Certainly not empty. It was full of framed photographs of family members, from both sides. No way would she look at them now! Definitely After The Move (ATM – ha!). Then she could divide them into 'His' and 'Hers' boxes, she thought sadly.

She'd need a chair to stand on, to put the suitcase back. As she walked through the lounge she stopped at the piano. No discussion about that! It was hers. Mum's old piano. This was one heirloom that she would continue to use and enjoy.

It was an upright with a lovely touch and tone. She could still see Mum playing her favourite Chopin waltzes. Alison had found the perfect place for it in the flat. Just as well it was an upright – no room there for a grand! She touched the keys, then sat down and started improvising a waltz of her own. She felt better; with her piano she'd never be lonely. And she'd sort out her sheet music ATM.

The girls had had piano lessons for several years, then had decided that swimming lessons would 'much more fun'. Later, of course, they'd regretted it and blamed Alison for allowing them to stop! A parent just can't win... She hoped that Gina and Gemma would have better luck with *their* children's music studies.

She wondered how the twins would feel about siblings younger than their own children. Would Mandy and the boys be happy with their new status? And how would they cope with another granny, similar in age to their mother? It really was a new world... She sighed. She'd been very happy with the old one.

At their fortieth wedding anniversary party Mark had repeated parts of his wedding speech. How could he have cast away his family so soon after? Apparently quite easily... After the estate agent's announcement, Alison had realised that solemn vows and gushing words could be abandoned at a whim. Who'd have thought that just a year after that party he'd leave his 'glamorous bride' for a mere child?

Why? Alison needed to find the real reason. Could it have been that he was simply bored with her? Had he been missing younger company since the twins had left home? Did he need to prove that he was still attractive? Did he need someone more pliable, someone who'd agree with him about everything? What had made him change so radically? Or had he just been gullible, enticed by the attentions of the younger, still-glamorous woman?

She hadn't looked around for a replacement during their marriage. There'd been some interesting, attractive possibilities, but she'd been content with her home, her work and her husband – blissfully ignorant of what was happening outside her own little world.

She went to the lounge and gazed at Gemma and Gina's wedding photos. *They* had been truly glamorous brides. In their wedding albums, still in the cupboard, were pictures of their tearful father walking his daughters up the aisle on their wedding days. (This was one day they were not going to share!) Mark hadn't ever needed any excuse to replay those videos, pausing on the brides, fast-forwarding past the guests! He had a good relationship with both his sons-in-law, and they enjoyed watching rugby and cricket together. But what now?

'Oh Joey, it's all too complicated? What shall I do?'

She felt her blood sugar dropping. Tea and sympathy were called for. Pam had said she'd be at home; she'd pop over there for a quick visit. Perhaps she'd even manage a slice of Pam's grated-chocolate cake.

Good thinking, said Joey. *Then I can sleep in peace.*

Those Were the Days

Margie had said that berries were good for the memory. Alison wondered if her sister was being unusually tactful, but she'd bought herself a punnet of raspberries anyway. Now she emptied them into a bowl, added yoghurt and admired the rich colours and textures. Not quite Wimbledon strawberries and cream, but just as delicious. A rare 'Thanks, Margie!'

As she savoured the fruit, Alison's mind turned to Mandy and her school project. What an incentive that was going to be – and just at the right moment! She could fill a book with stories of her childhood – and at the same time she'd clear the photos and newspaper cuttings. *And* she'd be doing her bit for the younger generation – dear Mandy! 'And in any case I need something to stimulate my little grey cells.'

Joey twitched an ear.

Alison finished the memory-reviving breakfast and strode purposefully to the photo cupboard. Without much trouble she found a huge envelope marked 'School Photos'. Thanks, Mum! What a relief not having to sort them! She took the box through to her bedroom and made herself comfortable on the bed.

How long since she'd opened this box? Did she actually need the photos? She'd kept in contact with several classmates, and as for the others, well, life goes on... Alison settled down on the bed. One last look won't kill anyone... and this was for Mandy...

At the top of the pile, a photo of the red-brick Victorian school building enclosing a D-shaped lawn – not to be walked on by young feet. Where rules unquestionably ruled! Alison closed her eyes and remembered...

The smell of old tea leaves that were used to clean the wooden floors... 'Why tea leaves?', they'd always wondered... The incessant buzz of the Christmas beetles – cicadas – in the trees, the scarlet and black 'lucky beans' that fell from the coral trees ('I must remember that's their proper name...') to be eagerly picked up for good luck in exams. The spitbugs' secretions that also fell from the trees, with a watery plop. Definitely less desirable than lucky beans! The 'itchy powder' from the plane trees, which the girls would try to push down each other's backs. Jacaranda blooms – pretty, but slippery – when the first flowers appeared they would know that exams were near... Christmas flowers – blue and pink hydrangeas – in enormous bowls decking the platform for prize-giving ceremonies.

The bus stop closest to the school was outside Oxenham's Bakery that enticed the children with garish gooey cream cakes, and sweets... Pink and white 'rock' – huge sugar crystals on a piece of string (what did that do to our teeth?), and four-for-a-penny um... (what do they call those balls these days?)

Made your teeth all black, for a bit... A block away, a funeral parlour, the hospital, and adjoining cemetery.

There it all was; the life cycle: birth, education and death, in one small area.

Alison gazed at a formal staff photograph. Her teachers were so last century – and more!

Not surprising, Joey rolled her eyes.

So different from Mandy's twenty-first century teachers whose clothes ranged from jeans and T-shirts, leggings and layered organza frills to shoestring 'tops' with unsynchronised bra straps. Pass the rescue remedy, please! Front row, centre, sat the headmistress, Miss Edwards. She had graduated from Cambridge, a real achievement in those days when few young ladies were accepted to study there. 'Why didn't we appreciate that?' Alison wondered. For much of the year, Eddie had dressed as if for a walk on the moors: tweed suit, grey or beige twinset, no pearls, sensible brogues. Mac and Donald, her two Scottie dogs, pattered behind her, the sound of their paws on the gravel path warning pupils and teachers alike that she was approaching. '*Cave!* She's coming!'

Eddie had insisted on 'the gells' speaking the Queen's English and even now Alison could barely say she was 'fine' without hearing Eddie's voice correcting her: 'The *weather* is fine, my deah; *you* are well.' Similarly, her gells did not 'swot' before exams, they 'revayzed'.

As a teacher herself, Alison now realised how difficult life must have been for Eddie. She had been almost a recluse, living in the school, and getting out only to go to church, or to an occasional concert with the gells. Perhaps she would have been accused of favouritism if she'd made friends with the teachers or the parents...? Her family lived in England and were seldom able to visit. How times had changed. Today school principals live with their families, on the school premises or in their own homes. Much healthier.

Alison studied the formal picture with surprise. Some of the teachers whom she'd thought of as 'ancient' were actually quite young, though others were definitely past retirement age. 'Like me! But it's all relative,' she grinned. What would *her* pupils say when they looked at their school photos forty years on?

Ally's teachers did not 'do' smiling in photos, and several of them, though possibly charming outside of the classroom, looked quite forbidding. 'We never thought of them as having home lives and families... To us the school was their life,' she thought sadly. Mrs Andrews, thin lips pursed in continual disapproval, sat upright as if her back were attached to an invisible rod. Years later, Alison heard that after a full day teaching Latin, Mrs Andrews would return home to care for her invalid husband. Sitting next to her in the photograph was asthmatic Miss Baines who had wheezed, coughed and spluttered her way through the mysteries of maths to the mainly uninterested girls.

'We couldn't have been much fun to teach,' Alison thought, 'but we were intrigued by Juffrou Bezuidenhout...'. There she was, in the back row, the pretty young Afrikaans teacher whose clothes seemed have come straight out of a fashion magazine. The only man in their school life had been an elderly history teacher, a lecturer from the university. Looking at the photo, Alison decided he couldn't have been more than forty!

And then there were the piano teachers. Miss Thomson, whose kitten ran along the keyboard – to her delight and the pupils' annoyance. Miss Cornelius, who took punctuality to an extreme – Alison could still hear the shrill screech of her alarm clock unmusically marking the beginning and end of each lesson. Strict Miss Harris, who later became Ally's mentor and friend. Most of her pupils practised diligently rather than be lashed by her sharp tongue: 'Go away, and come back when you've practised!' But she mellowed towards her pupils as they progressed, eventually treating them as young adults rather than naughty schoolchildren. They'd kept in contact all these years, but Miss Harris had never once suggested that Alison call her by her first name. 'Not like the camaraderie of today's teachers and pupils,' she thought wryly as she put the staff photo back in the box.

Numerous photos of Margie in various sports teams – school, provincial, even national... Sport was an important part of school life that had bypassed Alison. While she prayed that rain would cancel sport, Margie swam relentlessly through summer storms and ran miles every day. Their dad used to say that life began for Margie when the school bell rang for sport. Yet, despite being almost weighed down by the many sports' honour scrolls Mum had proudly sewn on her blazer, she still managed good academic results.

For Alison, school swimming had been a nightmare. Walking in 'crocodile' to the nearby public indoor pool with its sickly, musty smell. Sometimes the class went by bus to the huge open-air pool. She'd always been the last to change out of her cozzy and was terrified that the bus would go back to school without her. But soon the polio epidemic struck several children, and swimming in public pools had been restricted. The smell of over-chlorination still reminded her of those fearful days.

Sporting success for Alison had meant coming second-to-last rather than last in the school gala, but Gina and Gemma enjoyed sport, particularly swimming – and it was Margie's Graham who had preferred chess! How ironic that it was she, not Margie, who'd become the 'swimming mother', stopwatch ticking at galas and being Mom's Taxi for winter training! Of course she herself had preferred relaxing on the lilo at their pool at home, occasionally swimming a few strokes when it became too hot.

Alison's school had several tennis courts, the best and nearest to the school buildings being reserved for the top players. Naturally Alison and friends were always relegated to Court 4 – too far away for the coach to supervise their progress. Just as well: hidden behind a hedge, Court 4 faced the hospital entrance. The girls would bat the balls around for a few minutes then sit on the grass to watch the passing parade of doctors, nurses and ambulances. Far more interesting than searching for lost tennis balls!

These days Di was always nagging Alison to join her water aerobics class: 'You don't have to be a swimmer,' she'd encourage her. 'No one can see you! Your body's underwater. We're all too concerned with doing the exercises and enjoying the music to notice anyone else!' Hmmm...maybe After The Move – ATM?

Back to work! Her matric class photo! All of them so demure; feet, not legs, carefully crossed – the girls on the left crossing 'left over right' and those on the right doing the opposite. Who cared?

There'd been some characters in that class. The girl with the most unusual profession must have been Judy. Alison thought of the Springbok Radio show *Twenty Questions* in which the audience had had to guess the occupation of the contestants. She could hear the deep, resounding 'mystery voice' informing them that 'Judy is' – *long dramatic pause* – 'a chicken-sexer'. Her parents were poultry farmers, so it wasn't really such a curious choice.

Then Angela, looking so studious, her head perpetually bent over a book – only she was busy designing eveningwear, from elegant to outrageous. 'Such a conscientious student', agreed her teachers. Soon after she'd left school her Angelique label was high on the wish-list of many of Natal's society ladies! But after her marriage to a farmer, Angela had abandoned the world of fashion and started an arts and crafts centre for unemployed people in the area. Through her efforts, their work soon became sought after and sold both nationally and abroad.

Jackie was another one who'd done something worthwhile: recently retired as matron of a huge hospital, she presented papers at international conferences. And Vicky, the naughtiest girl in the class, was headmistress of their old school! But not all stories were as inspiring. Their dreams for Fiona, voted by the class to become an international model, crash-landed when she appeared on the back page of the *Sunday Times* as the mistress of a convicted fraudster. Alison and her friends hadn't known whether to be scandalised or impressed... And what did Miss Edwards think? Certainly not 'fine'.

Another classmate who made the headlines – front page this time – was Esmé, who'd educated her classmates politically. To the horror of her United Party parents, she joined the Communist Party while at university. Her phone had been tapped, and she'd spent time under house arrest. Soon after, she was smuggled out of the country to exile in Botswana. After 1990 she returned to South Africa and became involved in rural development.

The rest of the class had chosen less remarkable careers, mostly as teachers, nurses or secretaries. Sadly, as the years passed, their news had changed from marriage and perhaps divorce to ill-health and sometimes even dementia. They'd never thought that they'd be that old. Alison remembered watching grey-haired Old Gells, who'd come for Founders' Day, sitting on the school swings. They always sat on the swings, and they always talked about the same things:

'Don't go too high, Phyllis; we're not as light as we used to be!'

'Can you still play hopscotch?'

'Have a heart, Elaine! Not after my hip replacement!'

Alison and her friends had shaken their heads condescendingly. 'How pathetic! We'll never be like that!' Now here she was, taking a gentle swing down memory lane...

What had happened to the rest of them? She could try calling Stella on Skype; Stella kept in touch with everybody. And she'd take the photographs with her after all.

She closed the box and moved towards the kitchen.

'Joey, what shall we have for lunch?'

School... So many more memories... Where were her reports? Somewhere in a cupboard, along with the twins' reports. Hers were so old that they were almost Africana! It would be fun to compare the girls' reports with her own. She could probably even remember the teachers' different handwritings.

Alison sighed. Who *writes* anything today? Soon we won't be able to communicate in normal English – not unless they invent computers that can transcribe 'text' gobbledegook into 'proper' language. She liked that idea! But either way, the art of handwriting would soon be extinct. And SMS-ese would soon become another official language... 'Progressive' schools were no longer teaching cursive writing. How would her grandchildren sign documents? Perhaps in a giant step backwards they might revert to thumbprints!

Back in her own less frenetic schooldays they'd used pencils until Standard Three (Grade Five), when they proudly progressed to ink pens with nibs, G-nibs and Relief! These were dipped into Stephen's blue-black ink in an inkwell that sat in a small hole in each desk. Their fingers were perpetually stained and blotting paper was a necessity! In senior school they were allowed fountain pens, though those too could result in inky fingers. Alison had treasured her Conway Stewart pen for years. Ballpoint pens had been frowned upon and were forbidden at school as they 'ruined your handwriting.' They did too – her own writing was proof of that!

Alison was reasonably computer- and cellphone-literate – as long as the twins or their children were on call for help. She'd survived happily without Facebook, Berries, Pods or Tablets, and whatever else had been invented in the last twenty-four hours. She could make and receive calls and SMSes. What more did she need? No Tweet, Twitter or Twaddle, thank you.

Years before, Gina had sent her a cartoon showing an elderly woman resting her coffee mug in the CD holder of her computer. Not a bad idea, she'd thought! Her desk was so cluttered there was little space for refreshments.

Some of her peers had managed to bypass the computer age, while others had become IT fundis. Her friend Abby was truly scared of her machine and had permanently switched it off after she'd read a message saying: Do not ask this question again. Technology, like babies, was for the young or the strong-minded!

Alison resented the media describing people of sixty and over as 'elderly'. What nonsense! A popular woman's magazine had further insulted her age group by featuring clothes suitable for twenty- to fifty-year olds. Do we have to become mutton dressed as lamb, she thought, quite angrily, or are clothes of no importance to 'the elderly'? She pictured her friends in their cycling pants, leggings and even shorts, and in elegant evening wear, proving that there was life – and even glamour – for some, after fifty!

And cellphones? Alison had a love-hate relationship with hers. She needed one with large letters and numbers and used it only for phone calls and SMSes. One apparently used only ten per cent of one's brain; she used the same percentage of her cellphone functions. While not denying its value in an emergency, she resented its intrusion. That ringtone had Orwellian powers, taking precedence over everything. The friend who seconds before is chatting amiably to you in person, answers the imperious tune (often after much fumbling in pockets and handbag) and in mid-sentence ignores you in favour of the phantom caller. Sudden deafness afflicts her, and she acts as though everyone within a wide radius wants to share in her conversation.

'He *didn't*!'

'What did you *do*?'

'I should *think* so!'

Just a few weeks earlier, her friend Di, furious at being ignored for a Blackberry call, had ended a coffee date and possibly a friendship by walking out of a restaurant saying: 'Goodbye; let's meet again one day when you want to talk to *me*.'

Alison's all-time worst was watching two friends sitting together at a table in a coffee shop simultaneously talking vivaciously into their cells. Not to each other...

But cellphones could be useful, she supposed. Didn't they send out matric results to the learners' cellphones these days?

Matric results. 'Wasn't I looking for my school reports? Where could they be?' Alison's eyes lighted on a box on the top of the spare-room wardrobe. That was it! And a lot of other 'academic' bits as well. She heaved the box down, and scratched around in it until she found her own reports.

After reading too many that said 'Could try harder', she turned to the girls' reports. Why did nursery school teachers write in child-like script – it was the parents who read them, not the children! Gemma had enjoyed her peanut butter sandwiches and Gina had had difficulty tying her shoelaces! They hadn't spoken much in their first year at school, but, Alison smiled, they'd certainly overcome that problem!

It was time for the girls to keep their own reports (they could compare them with their own children's) and all this other stuff too. The university notes that Gina had thought she might use for further study one day... She'd ask – no, she'd *tell* – the girls to take away all their books and notes – and even their wedding photograph albums – and fill their own cupboards! I wonder what they'll do with *their* children's collections? Old enough to have their own children, old enough to store their own bits and pieces. The nest was empty, but their cluttering lingered on...

She and Mark had coped quite well with their empty nest: 'As long as the girls were happy,' they said. Both girls were working hard and kept in touch frequently. The 'forsaken parents' had to admit that they appreciated the extra space – and the freedom from the drama and upsets of teenage life. It was wonderful having the girls home for the holidays, catching up on news, having their friends in and out of the house and doing family things together: 'quality time' they called it these days. Their often-tiresome daughters had been replaced by lively, interesting, fairly sensible adults.

As parents they must have done something right. And it looked as if their children were on the right track too. She was really looking forward to helping Mandy with her project. She had so much material now!

'Material'? Is that what they call it now? Joey raised her eyebrows.

Take the 'A' Train

Alison took a stroll to the post-box at the top of the garden. She needed a break. Perhaps she'd find something there to take her mind off further decision making. But no luck: no post, only a flyer and some window-envelopes. 'Post' to her meant personal hand-written letters, or an invitation – both sadly rare these days. In her youth post came in pretty envelopes from girlfriends, or no-nonsense school-crested white from the current boyfriend. No texting or Facebook.

She dawdled back to the house as she looked at the flyer – these junk mail people had no thought of saving trees... She was beginning to sound like Margie.

Buy in bulk! Potatoes and onions! 10 kg packs! What about the single person? No decisions here for her! She folded the flyer into a paper plane and aimed it successfully at the garden bin.

As she walked into the house, the ring of her cellphone shattered her thoughts. Definitely not Margie time. Worse. A junk-call.

'You've been chosen as a lucky winner.'

'Oh yes?'

'A week's timeshare at blah blah blah... You need to come with your husband at 5 p.m.'

'You're divorced?' Abrupt change from previous saccharine-saturated tone. 'Then we can't offer this to you.'

End of call. Charming.

How insensitive, she thought. Is timeshare only for married couples? Did the same apply to men, she wondered? And common-law and same-sex couples? Call the gender-equality police or the new Consumer Protection Act?

Junk mail; junk calls; what about some junk food? She switched on the kettle.

Good attitude. Joey clearly approved.

She opened the freezer. One or two of the iced fairy cakes she was keeping for a special occasion? Now was definitely the moment. Just a few seconds in the microwave. First a pink one, then a white. 'Just what I need,' she justified herself, munching a chocolate one. ('They're miniscule, a mere nibble each,' she convinced herself.) Fairy cakes... cookies... cupcakes... even their name kept changing. Zoë had sent Alison a recipe for red velvet cupcakes! Whatever next?

All these changes were getting her down. She could do with a holiday... A luxury train! That's what she needed! Never mind Agatha Christie, the Orient Express was on her dream bucket-list!

She'd always loved train travel. The Orange Express! Stella and Alison travelling to Cape Town in the early 'sixties, a journey of two nights and a day. Best friends from childhood, they'd been through school together and now were off to university. A down-memory-lane chat was just what Alison needed, but Stella had emigrated to Seattle. It was after midnight over there.

Alison was amazed when she realised that her grandchildren had never been on a train. She'd promised them that they'd all go to Inchanga on the steam train as soon as she'd moved. She remembered how she and Mark had taken the twins to Umkomaas by train when they were Mandy's age. It had been such fun; they'd talked about it for years afterwards.

She reached for another fairy cake – might as well finish the pack; today was the sell-by date.

Even in today's world train travel was an adventure. Alison recalled the excitement as the train that was to take Stella and her to Cape Town swooshed into the grey Victorian station. The screeching of brakes, the piercing whistles and the general flurry while they watched their huge metal trunks being unceremoniously pushed into the goods van and then searched for their compartment among the printed name tags attached to the windows.

They'd had a coupé to themselves on that first journey! Emotional goodbyes, and then they were off! Within minutes of the waving hands disappearing from view they'd heaved the unwieldy windows closed and opened the life-saving raffia picnic basket that would sustain them for most of the journey. And those SAR breakfasts! Never since had hot toast seeped in butter and marmalade, and steaming coffee tasted so good!

The syncopated click-click rhythm that lulled us to sleep, the lush green of Natal giving way to the dry beauty of the Orange Free State. They sped past stations and sidings with curious names – Benoud, Hennenman, Bultfontein – then the Karoo, Olive Schreiner territory. Railway sidings for the farming communities: a platform, a water tank and perhaps two houses. Maritzburg was a bustling New York in comparison!

Later on more young people joined the train, laughing, waving goodbye to their families and excitedly greeting friends already on board. Obviously 'old' students, not first years like Ally and Stella. At dawn, the Boland and the Hex River Valley. Pale mauve mountains, vivid green vineyards, picturesque white farmhouses – like a De Jongh painting or a Joy Packer novel come to life. She'd never lost her love for the Cape.

Another delicious breakfast and they'd arrived in the Mother City! Then onto the suburban train. 'All stations; *alle stasies!*' Cape Town to Rosebank, past the vivid blue and purple morning glory blossoms that crept over the ugly fences along the railway line. How they'd loved the novelty of travelling to town by train! However, nothing could beat the once-a-term trip to Stella's grandmother in Muizenberg, where the railway line ran precariously along the edge of the sea.

Once you'd lived in 'the Fairest Cape' it would always feel like home. There was only one way to relieve the symptoms of home-sickness – she'd have to take the grandchildren to Cape Town!

A cup of rich hot chocolate and the remaining chocolate fairy cake! Now where were the Varsity photos?

After burrowing through more boxes and removing everything from the bottom shelf she found a mounted res photo, fortunately with the names of each of the two hundred girls. Some had come from as far as the Belgian Congo and South West Africa. Future doctors, politicians, dancers, scientists, teachers, musicians posed on the lawn in their white dresses and black academic gowns. Baxter Hall in its infancy.

Res life had been a culture shock for Alison. Sharing a 'flat', eating in the huge dining hall, presided over by the Lady Warden (appropriate title!). House committee, rules – so much to learn, even though Margie had warned her – greeting every member of the House Committee as Miss So-and-so and being called Miss Such-and-such yourself! The House Comm seemed almost as remote as their lecturers. Wearing an undergraduate gown for meals, taking care that the long bat-wing sleeves didn't fall into the soup! In winter most of them wore the gowns over their pyjamas for extra warmth.

Academic gowns were the official dress code for dinner and formal occasions. Students were not allowed to leave the dining hall until the final grace had been said. The only exception to that rule was to take a trunk call from home – parents knew their daughters would be in at mealtimes. In that case one had to stop for a solemn nod of 'permission to leave' from the Lady Warden. It was an ordeal, even without the worry of what might be happening at home that would have necessitated a long-distance phone call. The whole process was made worse in winter when one would have to walk the length of the dining room desperately clutching rolled-up pyjama pants to prevent them from descending to the floor! Alison still remembered the gales of laughter when Stella's pyjamas *did* fall down!

Their meals were served by waitresses, in black dresses with white caps and aprons. Formal dinners might include a guest speaker and we were all on our best behaviour. Pyjama pants very well-hidden!

Breaking rules had its penalties: an 'invitation' to attend House Comm meetings to explain why one had returned to res three minutes after midnight (one was 'gated' at one night per minute after midnight). Parents had to provide a list of family and friends whom the students were allowed to visit over weekends. By the next generation most of those customs were a thing of the past.

The highlight of the day was the arrival of the post. The anticipation was sometimes spoilt by Lettie, the 'lady in Lodge' (the entrance beyond which no male passed), calling out gleefully: 'No post for you, Miss So-and-so!' Alison's mother wrote to her every second day, always finding something to tell her about: the azaleas were in bloom, or a neighbour had 'flu…

Lettie used the new intercom system, proud to be technologically ahead of the other residences, to announce the arrival of 'gentlemen visitors'. The young women would often forget that that the intercom worked both ways, so the announcement was sometimes greeted with 'Oh no!' or 'Not yet!' or 'Tell him I'm out!' – all completely audible to the 'gentleman' concerned.

Despite the rules, men did occasionally enter the hallowed halls. Not always 'legally': on one occasion a few students from the nearby men's res got into a bedroom – no one would say how. A male invasion! Horrors! But there was little protest from the Baxter girls!

Such a lot of memories! Rag float-building night was another culture shock to Alison-from-Maritzburg. As a result of the amount of liquor consumed by the float builders during the night, several floats fell apart or were decapitated by the century-old oak trees en route to the parade through Adderley Street. One of them was the first ever College of Music float. Crazy days!

The music students had a set course: little choice of subjects – unlike most other students, who could choose to avoid first lecture! During winter, Alison's friend Emma hibernated in her res bedroom studying *Outspan* magazines and *Springbok Radio* serials, bolstered by chocolates, cigarettes and coffee. The weather was too miserable, she said – one could get pneumonia from walking to and from the campus. Saturday night dates, however, were not affected!

Alison picked up another photograph: students and lecturers in front of the lovely old College of Music building. She had been blown away by the fact that many of her lecturers were world-class professionals who frequently performed on the concert platform. She'd loved going by train with other students to the orchestral concerts in the City Hall on Thursday and Sunday nights. The evenings always finished with an intense post-mortem discussion over coffee, either at the café around the corner or back at res.

The College of Music was Alison's introduction to lecturers from Europe. Personalities and problems! Sonette, Alison's friend from a small dorp in the Karoo, had lived a very sheltered life in a conservative Afrikaans community. She barely understood English and was totally overwhelmed at her audition. She was interviewed by three lecturers, one German, one Italian and one Scottish. She told Alison that she'd just answered Yes and No in turn because she'd had no idea what they were asking her! They suggested she study the piano with Miss K, adding: 'You'll get on with her, she has a daughter your age,' *Miss* K – an unmarried woman with a daughter? Sonette was horrified. What sort of place had she come to! In tears, she walked up the stairs to Miss K's room, where she was greeted by: 'You poor child! You look as if you need a brandy!' When she got back to res her new friends had to explain to her about professional names and exaggerated figures of speech. She tried to understand.

Then there was the legend of two music lecturers meeting for the first time: on being introduced, one said: 'Can you do this?' and stood on his head. Without batting an eyelid, the other responded by instantly doing the same! Of such are friendships made!

She could dream on forever about those wonderful days...

There'd been some changes since her day of course. By the time Gina and Gemma were students, people of all races were accepted by the university and a more natural way of life had became the norm. And meals were no longer gender-segregated: the nearby men's residence provided meals for the Baxter girls as well – an economically and socially acceptable situation!

Thinking of how things had changed reminded Alison of the awkward moment when she'd enthused to one of her English lecturers, a world authority in his field, about a film that related to their studies. He hadn't been able to see it, he'd pointed out to her; he wasn't allowed into the cinema because he was 'Coloured'.

Then there'd been the frightening days Margie had told her about when the students had been confined to res as thousands of Africans marched to central Cape Town to protest against the killings at Sharpeville a few days earlier. Margie's friend June, unaware of what was happening in the 'real world', had bunked lectures and gone to town to buy a new mohair stole – very near to where the protest march was taking place. Margie had been frantic with worry until her friend strolled back from the station, totally oblivious of all the panic. Years later Gemma and Gina were forced out of lectures by protesting students who'd been burning tyres to try to block access to the campus. *C'est la vie…* Another era, another problem.

Such a lot to think about… she'd call Stella that night!

Back to the decluttering. But first, time for a break. At least she'd achieved something – she'd finally started on the photos.

Joey was unimpressed: *Two photos; big deal.*

Memories Are Made of This

Ring, ring… That darn phone again! Alison looked at her watch – Margie? Please, not. She could do with a diversion, but not a sisterly one.

Lucky again: 'Di! How lovely to hear you!'

'Just phoned to remind you about the college reunion lunch today. See you there!'

The what? She'd completely forgotten. Down-sizing was taking over her social life… The reunion! A valid reason to delay the daily decluttering ordeal, enjoy some pleasant company and a change of conversation! And no need to cook that evening. Bliss! Cooking for one was not Alison's favourite activity. Normally she didn't 'do' reunions, but today was different. Even Margie couldn't object!

Alison quickly changed out of her faded, comfy jeans and T-shirt and spruced herself up in a newish turquoise floral skirt and matching jacket. She didn't need any 'Oh poor Alison' comments from people she hadn't seen since the divorce. No time for a sassy haircut and tint to 'youthenase' herself! She would go as the confident, retired career woman rather than the discarded wife. Thank goodness she'd had her hair cut recently so she could easily brush it into some semblance of style. She did the best she could in the time left, dabbed on her special-occasion Fidji perfume, found the car keys in the grocery cupboard and rushed out of the house.

As she parked the car in front of the college she asked herself why she'd accepted the invitation. Then, remembering the alternative, she skipped up the steps. The buildings did their usual trick, looking smaller and shabbier than they had when she'd been a student there. She stopped at the front door, took a deep breath, and forced herself into the noisy room. Shrieks of welcome reassured her. 'They still recognise me! I can't look *that* bad!'

A couple of pre-lunch cocktails later and she was in the forefront of updating news and backdating stories – many boldly exaggerated for optimum effect. 'I really am enjoying this,' she confessed to herself with surprise. 'It's good to be back in the real world!'

Alison found herself in a group discussing how easily pupils could forget their teachers.

'Tell me about it,' Alison laughed, 'I had a really embarrassing incident, years ago. One of Mark's clients invited us to dinner at his mansion – it was an amazing *Top Billing*-type place. Mark loved these functions, but they weren't my scene at all.

'When we got there I begged him not to leave me alone, but of course he did! So I just stood there, for ages – well, I suppose

it was only a few minutes really – longing for a familiar face...
And then, like an answer to a prayer, there was Roy Lang –
remember Roy Lang, the successful entrepreneur?'

'I was *so* relieved! I told the hostess that she didn't need
to introduce us and that we went back all the way to when
I taught him at Carlton Junior! Roy was the Pirate Captain
when I directed *The Sailor's Tale*, so we knew each other well
then. I was so relieved at knowing someone at the party that
I sang the opening phrase of the title song right there! Can
you imagine! And of course the guests gathered round to hear
more about high-flyer Roy as a young star.

'It was terrible! Roy just looked me up and down with a supercilious frown and said "You must be mistaken. I have no
recollection of you – or the play..."' Alison put on a pompous
voice.

'And then? What happened?' 'What did you do?' Di and Liz
spoke simultaneously.

'It was too awful; I didn't know what to say. There was this
really awkward silence. The poor hostess tried to rescue the
situation by saying something like "Do try some of my mushroom croquettes while they're still hot." It didn't help much
though...'

'So what *did* you do?' Liz again.

'Nothing! I didn't know *what* to do. I wished I could rush off
like the White Rabbit, to a very important date... I just went on
standing there. I guess I took a mushroom croquette!'

Everyone laughed. Alison felt happy to be the centre of
attention with her sad little story.

'Where was Mark all this time?' Caroline had just joined the
group.

'Oh, he was totally unaware, chatting to some business
friends around the bar. But that wasn't the worst of it. Later in
the evening Roy came up to me and said, "I do remember you
now." Can you imagine how I felt!'

Her friends shared her indignation.

'How magnanimous!'

'I'd have kicked him!'

'He's always been an arrogant prig.'

'Even more so since he became a partner in that prestigious firm...'

'That's one evening I'd rather forget...'

'Hmm, I've also made the "forgettable list",' Caroline consoled her. 'I had this pupil called Melanie – she was a jolly "who's-for-hockey, chaps?" kind of girl. But her essays, oh, her essays – talk about creative spelling! And an almost total absence of punctuation...' Caroline shook her head, remembering. 'Anyway, years later my friend Claire tells me that her new neighbour is this same Melanie, and that she's now a regular contributor to *Popular Woman* magazine. I was flabbergasted! Can you imagine! Then Claire insisted on inviting us both to her home for tea and reminiscences. Actually I was quite looking forward to seeing Melanie again, and then I could catch up on news of her classmates. I liked them; they were a lively bunch. 'So anyway, a few days later Claire phoned me and said "Melanie says she'd love to come for tea but she doesn't remember you at all." Same story...'

'Did you go?' asked Liz.

'You must be joking! Of course not!'

'Well, at least you weren't snubbed to your face in public,' said Alison wryly.

'Did you ever read any of her articles?' Erna asked.

'Of course I did!'

'And?'

'They were interesting – and even quite well written!'

'Thanks to spellcheck and editors,' laughed Erna.

During the lunch, which was remarkably tasty and generous, the conversation returned, not surprisingly, to teaching tales.

'Did I ever tell you about my first day at my first permanent post?' Liz asked. 'What a disaster! I had to play the piano to accompany the hymns at Assembly. So the previous day I checked on which hymn book they used. I was relieved to see the piles of blue *Hymns of Praise* on the shelf. So on the first real day of term, the headmaster announced the hymn number, and I played the introduction. Utter silence. My solo performance petered out after a few bars of course, and then a high-pitched voice called out: "We don't use the blue hymn book. It's number whatever in the red book!" I hadn't noticed the red ones in the cupboard! I just wanted to sink through the floor. My first day and the whole school thought I was a complete idiot.' Liz shuddered at the memory.

Frank joined in. 'Your first day – my last day! The farewell ceremony at Brentwood Training College – let me tell you about that.'

'What happened?' 'Yes, do tell us.' Alison and Caroline were eager to hear of someone else's bad experience.

'Well, at the final Assembly the head student always says a few words of thanks to the leaving staff and presents them with farewell gifts. There we are, all sitting on the stage, waiting to be called up. All the other leavers were acknowledged and thanked and given their farewell gift. But nothing for me.'

'How come?'

'What did you do?'

'What could I do? I just sat there on the stage pretending I wasn't there. I could hardly have put up my hand and said, "And me? Give me my gift!" Anyway eventually the head student noticed the remaining ownerless gift... There was this embarrassed silence on the stage – and lots of muted chattering from the students. Confusion. Then a whispered discussion with the Rector... And all the time I'm just sitting there. Eventually the penny dropped and I was thanked and invited to receive my present. And after all that it was just a stupid mug with the college crest on it.'

'Your favourite mug now, huh?'

'But it was just an unfortunate oversight,' commiserated Bruce.

'Yes, perhaps, but a major one when it's you! It certainly made me feel okay about leaving!'

Tom took over. 'I know how you must have felt. I learnt the

hard way about my place in the pupils' hearts. I thought they'd be upset when I left after five years and I put off telling them for as long as possible.'

'And so? What did they say when they heard?'

'They just said: "Who's going to take your place?" I was really upset.'

'So much for loyalty.'

'Yes, but I did learn something.' Tom looked thoughtful. 'Since then I've tried to express my appreciation to those who have meant a lot to me while they are still around – and still alive! Sometimes we don't show how we feel, and then it's too late…'

Alison nodded; Tom was right. Her thoughts went back to Carlton Junior and the Afrikaans teacher who had supported and encouraged her when she was young and inexperienced. 'Time I visited you, Miffie; I need to tell you how much I learned from you…'

It was getting dark before the stories and reminiscences finally came to an end, and they reluctantly said their farewells, promising to meet again soon. 'Then we'll talk about the good times!' promised Di.

'Good, bad, anything, as long as we can laugh about them!' Liz grinned.

'And as long as we can still remember them!'

Alison was in good spirits as she arrived home. Joey greeted her accusingly: *That was a remarkably long lunch*.

Alison switched on the kettle.

'Who would have thought that a teachers' reunion could be such fun! And not a word the whole afternoon about decluttering! I'll take the evening off, Joey, and get cracking on those photos for Mandy early tomorrow.'

You're such a good story teller. Joey winked.

Friends and Neighbours

Alison had been looking forward to having her two young grandsons for the morning, but Gina had phoned to say that she'd forgotten they had to go to a birthday party. Alison was disappointed; the boys' constant questions made her aware of how quickly the world was changing, and she always enjoyed their boisterous company.

A glance at the newspaper, a quick cup of coffee – and then down to work.

The horoscope must have been written specifically for her: 'This is the week for action. No more procrastinating. Lower your stress levels by doing what has to be done.'

It couldn't be more explicit. She'd added nothing to the Out-box yesterday. And there was Mandy's project.

So – the photos! Out with the duplicates, the blurred, the headless, the limbless. 'I can do it! For Mandy I can do it!' she shouted enthusiastically to a mildly startled Joey. She opened the cupboard bulging with photos and picked up the album that immediately fell at her feet. She moved to the lounge and sat down next to Joey. Her childhood album of Maritzburg, many years ago…

On the first page: her Mum and Dad, with their next-door neighbours Aunty Hetty and Uncle Hardy, under the jacaranda tree at home.

Hardy was actually their surname. Somehow Margie and Ally had never called him Uncle George. Alison's grandchildren were confused by the fact that older friends of the family had been called Aunty or Uncle as a form of respect and affection. Why? Many of *their* friends called their parents, even their grandparents, by their first names.

Alison turned the photo over. On the back, in her mother's handwriting: Gordons and Hardys. Even the captions were formal.

Aunty Hetty was a Scottsville personality. In the photograph she was wearing her favourite blue floral shirtwaister dress with scalloped Peter Pan collar, and a matching blue cardigan with bobbles – high fashion! Alison's mind wandered still further… Peter Pan might have worn a similar collar, but surely not scalloped?

The Hardys had lived in their Maritzburg-style red-brick, tin-roofed house for fifty years. Alison smiled as she thought of the 'living room', a euphemism if there ever was one, as the room was seldom used and certainly never 'lived' in. It was enshrined in the dark: 'We don't want the sun to fade the curtains do we, George?' – and opened only to the doctor, the clergy and, at worst, death. On the rare times that she'd peeped into the lounge, Alison had been saddened by the three china ducks stuck on the wall, flying nowhere, forever.

She and Margie asked their mother why Aunt Hetty hid the arms and backs of the faded green Sanderson lounge suite with beige crocheted antimacassars. Why cover them up when no one ever sat there to make them dirty!

Dear Aunt Hetty! Perched on a ladder, her garden hat at an angle to ward off the sun, she'd cut the hedge armed with shears, determination and a Federer-sharp eye contradicting a line-call. When comparing the Hardy's perfect lawn with their own undisciplined weed-friendly one, Alison's mum would comment indignantly, 'Well, no weed would *dare* grow there!' Even their poppies and Barberton daisies stood up straight.

Margie and Ally were fascinated by the Hardys' chickens, forever squawking in their *hok* in the backyard. Aunt Hetty had little sensitivity about eating a juicy friend for Sunday lunch: 'That's what they're there for, aren't they, George?'

' Yes, dear,' he'd reply, sadly.

Alison's family was more conventional, with only a dog and cat. At least you could cuddle and play with them, and you weren't expected to eat them later.

Uncle Hardy had a car, ancient even in those days, with a dickey seat at the back. Very occasionally he'd let Margie and Ally sit in that extra seat where the boot should be, and drive them around the block. That was a real treat!

Alison remembered Aunt Hetty speaking authoritatively in microscopic detail on any topic, from making jam 'the right way' and how the city should be run to the 'goings-on' at the Women's Institute meetings. Although childless, she readily dispensed advice on friends' parenting problems: 'It's just common sense!'

Uncle Hardy, on the other hand, was a quiet man – 'Did he have an option?' Alison's dad would laugh. His conversation was largely limited to 'Yes, dear' and 'Of course, dear' in agreement with his over-chatty wife. She drew him into the conversation with comments such as: 'I caught the 7.50 bus, didn't I, George?' 'Yes, dear,' he'd reply. 'It *was* the 7.50,' she'd continue with barely time for a breath, 'because I hung up the washing and chopped up the veggies for lunch then just as the clock struck seven thirty Emily phoned with news of the new grandchild. I had to cut her short and rush off to catch the bus, didn't I, George?'

'Yes, dear,' he'd answer dutifully.

On her return from town Aunt Hetty would systematically unpack her shopping, commenting colourfully on the price – high or a bargain – the attitude of the cashier, the punctuality of the bus and snippets of gossip about the passengers. Then she'd switch on the kettle and collapse into her chair: 'Just in time for *From Crystal with Love*, aren't I, George?'

'Yes, dear.'

Alison returned momentarily to reality. 'When was the last time I caught a bus?' she wondered.

Because her parents had never owned a car, travelling by bus had been the norm. The early morning bus had been a significant part of her life from kindergarten to matric. Travelling by bus was more than merely transporting passengers from one part of town to another. It was a way of life.

Alison's dad was a regular 7.50 passenger every workday for thirty years. He would greet the driver and conductor – in those far-off days there was a conductor who sold and clipped the tickets – and slip into 'his' seat, nodding in greeting to the other passengers.

Topping the passenger chat-list were personal curiosity (aka prying) – in the nicest possible way, of course; the weather, inclement or merely seasonal; the arrival of the bus, punctual or not; and the latest episodes of their favourite radio serials.

Almost all the passengers were regulars; any newcomer was greeted with raised eyebrows. Discovering their identity provided a welcome topic of discussion. The more curious passengers hoped that the newcomer would sit next to Aunt Hetty, who would don her investigative hat and start 'the interrogation'. The chatter of the passengers decreased to a pianissimo in an effort to hear some of the cross-examination.

No desperate attempt of the suspect to view the passing scenery or to read a novel would deter the Maritzburg Miss Marple!

The arrival of spring produced a special excitement. As the bus reached the Umsinduzi River bridge the passengers would crane forward and then twist to the left to catch sight of the huge oak tree that spread its branches out across the road. Murmurs of pleasure would ripple through the bus at the sighting of the first leaves. Aunt Hetty had even seen Major MacTavish secretly raise his eyes above the page and give a terse nod of approval before resuming his re-reading of the local headlines.

Decades ago Alison had thought of returning to Maritzburg just to catch the bus again – if it still went along that route. The passengers would certainly have been different; most of the older ones pushing up daisies, as her mum would have said.

Wednesday was an important day for Alison's dad. Early in the morning he'd buy fruit and vegetables for the family and the neighbours at the market adjoining the bus terminus and go off to his business. The kindly porters would store his purchases until lunch time. As the City Hall clock struck midday and the little figures came out of the clock to perform, the bus bound for Scottsville would arrive at the terminus. Dad's bargains were brought out and taken onto the bus by a porter who would stack them in the parcels area under the staircase. Alison's dad would arrive a minute or two later, board the bus, check the contents of the boxes and give the driver a nod, signalling 'permission to depart'. When they arrived at 'his' bus stop, the conductor would help him offload the boxes and place them on the bench. Then he'd wave the bus on its journey and walk home down the road. Passing residents would note the unattended boxes and nod sagely: 'Mr Gordon's been to market!'

His arrival at home was the signal for Joseph the gardener to grab the wheelbarrow, while reluctantly accepting a bright floral sunshade from Alison's mum – she would not be responsible for Joseph's getting sunstroke from the fierce midday heat. Soon Rutland Road residents would be treated to the sight of Joseph, flourishing the sunshade, one-handedly steering the wheelbarrow on which the bargains of the week were precariously bouncing! After work the neighbours would come to the house and divide up what Gina used to call 'Grampa's vegables'.

Alison sipped the last drops of her now lukewarm tea and sighed, 'It could only have happened in Maritzburg.' As she emptied the cup she added: 'and in the 'fifties.'

At ten o'clock every Boxing Day morning ('Now it's the Day of Goodwill; even holidays have new names,' thought Alison) the Gordons would troop over to the Hardys for a formal tea. They were welcomed onto the red-polished back stoep, decorated with overhanging wooden 'broekie lace', where tea was served on the best willow-pattern plates. Margie and Alison would perch gingerly on the edge of the cane chairs, on perfectly sewn floral cushions.

They'd loved Aunt Hetty's Boxing Day teas: scones, mince pies and a beautifully decorated Christmas cake – she'd used the same recipe for Alison and Mark's wedding cake. 'I can't count how many prizes I've won for that cake. Can you, George?'

'No, dear,' he'd reply, as expected.

Years later, before Margie became health conscious, the sisters would research the best mince pies in town. Aunt Hetty's really were hard to beat.

Mince pies? Real mince any time. Fruit mince? Never! Joey licked her lips.

Aunt Hetty was a believer in positive re-enforcement. Those who impressed her were rewarded with delicious biscuits that she'd made at five o'clock that morning.

'Best time for baking, isn't it, George?'

'Yes dear,' he'd sigh from behind his newspaper.

She cared for him through his final illness, and afterwards, when her eyes failed, she moved to a retirement home. 'I'm going to enjoy every moment! Sheer waste of time thinking what might have been!' They half expected to hear the familiar 'Yes dear,' but that was 'what might have been'.

'Where have all the characters gone?' sighed Alison as she returned the photo to the album. No one, not even Margie, would make her destroy these precious pictures of the past.

She'd review more photos another time. She stood up.

Oh for Aunt Hetty's mince pies! Or anyone's mince pies! Alison opened the grocery cupboard. A Marie biscuit would have to do.

She telephoned Margie. 'I've been going through the photos.'

Joey opened her eyes, querying the plural form.

'D'you think *we'll* ever be described as interesting characters? Or do they belong to a lost generation?'

'Typical Alison,' laughed Margie, 'I'm sure every generation has them; one just has to have time to reminisce! I'll phone you back later, I'm busy kneading bread!'

Bread! Alison had been too engrossed in her memories to notice that it was past lunch time.

Never been known to happen before. Joey looked amazed.

The Song is Ended

Only the week before, Alison had spoken to Caroline about visiting their old colleague, Iris, at the Groenfontein retirement home. Iris had taken them under her wing when they were young and inexperienced teachers at Carlton Junior. 'As soon as I've moved to the flat,' she'd said.

Now here was Caroline again. And it was too late. Like Tom had said at the reunion...

They didn't talk for long.

After they'd rung off, Alison stood quite still, not sure of what to do. After a while she went to the photo cupboard and rummaged around until she found the Carlton school photos.

She walked slowly to the lounge and sat down on the couch. Joey, sensing her mood, moved onto her lap.

Iris had always been known as Miffie. She was the Afrikaans teacher, and 'Miffie' was short for *mevrou*. She'd resigned from a previous teaching post after an incident when she believed that the school board had behaved unethically towards a colleague. She refused to mention the school by name, merely pointing her thumb over her right shoulder as she spat out the words, 'when I was over there'.

Miffie was proud to be a teacher of 'the old school' who taught her pupils grammar rules by rote. None of that new-fangled 'let's play games' method. Teaching is not a joke. Your pupils' careers depended on it.

'Don't think that I wave a magic wand and whoops, your children become *tweetalig*. It takes hard work, drumming rules into those empty heads! You parents think that just by you paying a lot of money and your sons sitting in my classroom they'll absorb the language by osmosis! *Nee wat!* Educating children is a three-way business. You, me and the child!' Miffie was adamant.

When certain 'progressive' parents confronted the headmaster about Miffie's 'archaic methods', he'd confidently reply: 'Well, her results speak for themselves! It's thanks to Miffie that your son will be accepted at the high school of your choice.' Miss Edwards would have approved, thought Alison.

Then there were the Parents' Evenings! Alison wasn't sure who'd dreaded them more, the children or the parents. While few parents bothered to see Alison about their children's music progress, the queues outside the Afrikaans classroom snaked around the corner; no parent dared miss an appointment with Miffie. And when they reached the head of the queue, *they* didn't interview *her*… The children knew that she'd tell their parents exactly what they had or hadn't done in class, and parents sometimes wished they'd checked their children's homework as scrupulously as they'd searched for their own photographs in the social pages of the newspaper.

Iris was the daughter of a minister in a poor community in the Karoo. She knew about poverty, hardship and – especially – the importance of education. Her father's salary had been reduced when her mother died, the church council declaring that there was one less mouth to feed. She'd rush home from school at break to prepare the midday meal for her father and her siblings. She mended and cleaned their clothes, saved from church jumble sales. After matriculating, Iris had worked as a filing clerk to pay for her first year at training college. After that she'd won bursaries that allowed her to complete the course.

When Iris became a teacher 'Waste not, want not' remained her motto: she'd examine the schoolboys' old exercise books and tear out any blank pages for re-use; used envelopes were recycled for notepaper, and nonchalant comments of: 'My mum will buy me another book tomorrow' were absolutely unacceptable. Similar comments about lost cricket bats or school-bags would elicit a brusque 'Look for it *again* at home – and check Lost Property – before you dare ask for more! Money doesn't grow on trees!' *Liewe wêreld!* What did their parents teach them?

In the staff room Miffie would entertain her younger colleagues – Alison among them – with her legendary *melktert*, and pithy comments about her 'old boys'. She had some pithy comments for the boys too: 'Come Christmas you'll be crying in your cradle!' – a dire warning that their work was not up to her high standard, and 'You're just like your dad! Not stupid, just bone lazy!'

Miffie hadn't pulled her punches, but she'd had an understanding of each child that made them try their best to please her. Alison sighed; she'd learnt so much from Miffie... She'd help any child with their Afrikaans after school for no extra payment. 'Some need more time and individual attention,' she'd say. 'It's my job to see that he understands.'

Alison felt so guilty. Why hadn't she phoned Miffie for cheery chats? It was ages since she'd visited her in the box-like room at the retirement home in the centre of town. She'd looked tiny and frail, in the institution-type iron bed covered with a colourless candlewick bedspread. On the wall hung several sombre Biblical pictures, and the small table was cluttered with class photographs of 'her boys'.

She'd greeted Alison with delight. 'Let's not talk about me', she whispered, waving away Alison's query as to her health. 'Let's rather talk about my boys.' Alison passed her one of the photographs from the table. '*My wêreld!* The good, the bad and the ugly! *Ag*, they were real characters, weren't they?' Alison knew that Miffie had loved them all...

You were the unforgettable character, Miffie. You'll never know the influence you had on so many pupils, friends, colleagues...

Alison returned the photos to the cupboard. Enough of the past for one day.

Sunrise, Sunset

The news of Miffie's death had changed Alison's mood. Why hadn't she done more, visited or phoned regularly? She started wondering about who would sort out *her* papers when *she* was gone. Mandy's project was far from her mind now.

Alison had a fear of official documents; Mark had taken care of those. 'I must get organised,' she said to herself, 'the least I can do is make things easier for the girls. I'll make an appointment with Rob to update my will, and check that everything's in order. The girls need to know where everything is; they shouldn't have additional stress. I'll get rid of all the unnecessary papers and clutter later.'

Isn't that what you're doing anyway? Joey moved her head quizzically.

Alison looked warily at the boxes in the cupboard. Not the photos – she'd do those properly, soon, for Mandy. But somewhere in that mess was a box with all the cards, letters and telegrams commemorating family occasions. She'd kept them all; they were the family history! One day the grandchildren would want to know about their roots, and be grateful that she'd kept them. Not exactly the *Who Do You Think You Are?* television programme, where celebrities delved back into their own histories, but she'd do her best with her limited resources.

Of course she'd need time to research all the family events and re-live the happy and sad times. Perhaps it could turn into a future project – she wanted something to do. She could produce something really worthwhile that the children and grandchildren would cherish as their heritage. Mandy's project could develop into a real family history... After the move she'd be more relaxed and be able to complete the job. Maybe she could even find someone who'd want to publish it; a kind of 'period piece'.

Joey grinned: *Will I be famous?*

Back to work. The desk in the study. She opened the lid, and was greeted by an assortment of wrapping paper of all sizes. Some were really minute. What on earth could be wrapped in such small scraps? Be sensible, Alison, turf them out! And this? Labels, already recycled from the charity shop. Out! And all these pretty paper packets? So useful! She tried to straighten them out. Even ironing wouldn't help... And these cards? So that's where she'd put them.

Be brave and throw them all out.

She took a deep breath and stuffed them into the bin. Progress, she smiled! On second thoughts, she rescued the packets – some could really be used again.

Fifty percent success, sniffed Joey.

When Miffie was at Groenfontein she'd enjoyed recycling old cards for charity; they were always asking for cards. 'I could take my boxes to them…once I've been through them all.' (*Next century?* Joey blinked.) 'They'll never advertise for cards again. And the grandchildren will have the memoir instead.'

The letters from Mark, written when they were courting – Out! That was easy! It would be hurtful to re-read them. We had some good times, she thought wistfully… But obviously not enough for him. On the other hand, maybe they'd give a clue as to his puzzling behaviour…

What was this dusty roll of papers at the back of the cupboard? The kids' letters and paintings? No way would she let those go – they'd cheer her up when she was old and really grey! Ah, this one! – an early Gina, done after a gala when her team had come third. Although they were standing on the lowest box of honour to receive their medals, Gina had drawn them twice the size of the winning team!

Thinking about swimming reminded Alison of beach holidays in Durban… There must be snaps of them somewhere… Alison rummaged around for a bit… Success! Here's one of Margie, and self-conscious Alison, leaning against the north beach wall, where the confident local teenagers arranged themselves to view and be viewed by the passing 'talent'! Both sisters had been too shy to wear an 'itsy bitsy teeny weeny yellow polka dot bikini' – even though those bikinis covered almost as much as regular one-piece costumes! Alison had felt like a real teenager in her halter-neck cozzy with frills around the hips. Mandy would love those! And what was this? One of those ghastly cards where you put your head through the picture of the fat lady. Can definitely go! Into the bin.

Alison was too nervous to look through the desk in the study. Mark was right on that point: her idea of tidying was merely to move things from one drawer to another. Diaries from years back, personal phone books, ditto; their wedding gift book – that would make interesting reading once she was settled in the flat… ATM, yes.

Forget the nostalgia and think of the future. But that didn't excite her either. ATM she'd make a 'bucket list'; not now.

Di wanted to go bungee jumping and hang-gliding; she felt safer on land. She preferred her idea of writing a book for her grandchildren – and great-grandchildren – there'd be some, some day... She had plenty of material... Unless she wrote a novel – about a divorce! But maybe not: defamation cases were expensive and there'd be no point publishing posthumously...

A cup of coffee and a cinnamon rusk later, and Alison was ready for the fray. Back to the cupboard cleansing.

Alison removed an old chocolate box, the cover picture a faded Swiss mountain scene, from the top shelf. Yellowed newspaper cuttings that *Mum* couldn't throw away! 'Don't blame me,' sighed Alison, 'it's obviously a genetic problem...'

Stiff, stilted wedding pictures from past eras, so different from today when they're often taken after the event, barefoot on the beach or wading in the sea in their expensive wedding clothes! The social page of the local newspaper from 1946 included detailed descriptions of the clothes worn by the entire retinue. A bride had to be as strong as Tromp van Diggelen to carry such a gigantic bouquet! 'If she'd dropped it on her foot she'd be immobile,' thought Alison flippantly. No wonder brides of that era usually looked so solemn. Unlike Gina who'd giggled down the aisle: 'My garter's slipping!'

She came across a newspaper article about a cousin's wedding that included a list of wedding gifts and their donors. Good heavens! That was worse than publishing exam results for all to read! In those days guests who travelled to Maritzburg from as far afield as Camperdown made news! Not like today's young people who seemed to travel round the world to friends' weddings as regularly as their parents went to the supermarket.

Death notices too – formal, serious and impersonal. No cheery last messages to the departed as in today's columns: 'Cheers! Will down a few drinks for you!' or 'We'll miss you on Fridays at the pub!' Alison hoped that those mourners had told the departed what jolly good fellows they were when they were alive. She couldn't get Miffie out of her mind. There was so much she wished she'd said...

What will they write about me? No trite or poetic comments, thank you. Don't wait till I'm dead; tell me now! Who would miss me? Margie, for a start. They'd had their moments even though the age-gap didn't always make it easy. They didn't quite live up to the sugary song 'Sisters, Sisters, There Were Never Such Devoted Sisters', but there was a bond, and they were there for each other when needed. Yes, Margie really cares. Her decluttering list had proved quite useful and she'd offered to come to Durban to help her.

Her children? She certainly hoped so! Had she been a good mother? She'd tried! She'd enjoyed schlepping them to all their activities, though not the crazy 5 a.m. swimming training! She who hated swimming almost as much as she hated getting up early! The Alison form of *mater*dom (*A Latin joke!* Joey was impressed), not the 'Tiger Mother' Amy Chau method of parenting. 'But they were happy, I think,' she nodded to Joey who stared back, unimpressed. 'And look how well *you've* been treated,' she added meaningfully.

Hospitable? Their home was always open to all the children's friends. They'd lived close to the school so it had become the Safe House for parents to collect their offspring if either were running late. And on inter-school sports weekends the dining room would be so chock-a-block with kids that she and Mark would have to eat their lunch in the kitchen! Those were great days! He'd seemed happy then...

She must remind Gemma and Gina to enjoy being 'Mom's taxi' before their own children started driving and those years...dwindled into a fond memory. Would the little ones remember her 'granny stories' – some true, some imagined? They'd had such fun together. And there'd be more! She wasn't planning on departing just yet. Too many memories to make... It seemed only yesterday that the twins were babies.

Because they were twins everyone, from Aunt Becky (naturally) to Johnny the fruit and vegetable vendor, had felt obliged to advise on their upbringing. Mark had bought *How to Cope with Twins* (the cover showed two shrieking toddlers throwing toys at each other, and the mother blocking her ears in desperation). The book was more depressing than helpful and they'd abandoned it after reading the chapter on *Psychotic Twins*. They'd just trusted to instinct and hoped that their twins would grow up reasonably normal.

When the girls were ready to start 'big school', Alison and Mark were flooded with advice from people who hadn't had twins – or in several cases, even children – on whether they should be sent to the same school. But the thought of different uniforms, teachers, sports events, friends and parties was too much even to consider. As Mark's mother sagely commented: 'Every pair of twins is different, so surely there can't be any hard and fast rules?' The only advice they'd followed was that of Mark's father: 'Why look for problems? If a problem arises, then that's the time to start worrying about it.' That made sense!

Once, when Gina and Gemma were discussing their child-hood with Alison and Mark, they'd admitted to enjoying their schooldays but, on thinking back to their school dance, they'd chanted in unison: 'How *could* you have let us wear those dresses?' Alison reminded them it was their choice entirely! If that had been their only problem, she could relax!

Would they remember her cooking, she wondered. Not that she'd seen any comments on cooking in obituaries! She'd read somewhere that cooking was a way of showing one's love for one's family… After that tentative start, she'd become a reason-ably good cook, with a few specialities. And the girls still asked for her recipes; that was a good recommendation! Alison seldom stuck to recipes; she would use whatever was in the grocery cupboard. 'Variations on a theme' she called it. So the snoek pie became a mackerel one – no bones to remove; the apple cake changed to apricot – tastier, and unusual! Nine out of ten for imagination plus practicality! Margie, being vegetarian, had a reputation for the healthiest food in the family – she'd used organic ingredients before they became popular and environ-mentally correct. But the twins always insisted that they stop at The Bakery in Maritzburg after lunch at Aunt Margie. And

Margie's son, Graham, usually had two helpings of Alison's comfort food – as long as Margie wasn't around!

Back to the task! The good wife? Apparently for four decades only… But it takes two to tango, she consoled herself. She was not agonising along that route today. She was resilient; she gave herself full marks for outwardly surviving Mark's bombshell. Fortunately the girls had the support of their husbands, and were busy with their own families. It was quite possible that Floozy would want her own child. How would they cope with the arrival of a sibling – younger than their own children?

Alison tried not to criticise Mark in front of the twins, and they were sensitive enough not to discuss his Sandton lifestyle in her presence. And all this without a nervous breakdown or a therapist! 'I could become a motivational speaker!' she giggled.

Dream on, yawned Joey. *You're the one who needs motivation or there'll be no ATM.*

Alison loved teaching and had been happy in all her jobs, though of course some schools had been better than others. 'I was so lucky to have chosen the right career…' she'd often say. What could be worse than getting up each day to face a job one didn't enjoy? She loved hearing from former pupils spread all over the world – though the humorous 'Greetings to our *old* teacher' were getting too close for comfort! 'What will *they* say about me when I'm gone?' The cloudy obituary theme returned.

'I think I'll phone a friend.'

She dialled Di's number. 'Hi, Di! What will you remember about me when I'm gone?'

'What? What's wrong? Are you ill?' Di sounded worried. 'You looked fine at the reunion…?'

'It's not my health. I'm tired, and I'm depressed, my back is aching, and I need sleep. But it's none of that; it's the wretched decluttering. Reading all those old family obituaries has thrown me into morbid mode. You know what happens to people when they retire…'

'Is that all?' Di was relieved, 'Research shows that sixty is the time for a new career path. You're overdue for a change, my friend! You could teach from home. Or if you're sick of teaching you could become a librarian – you love books, Ally. Or there's always bridge! It's such a social game, you'd never be lonely.'

'Oh, come on; I've got no card sense; you know that. Remember how dreadful I was when we both started those lessons years ago? I never understood how everyone else could remember the cards, in and out, and all that. And the calling – that was like a secret language everyone understood except me!'

'If only you'd persevered,' sighed Di. She brightened: 'There's always kaluki. Lots of fun and not too hard on the brain.'

'Kaluki? Thanks, but no thanks! In any case I've got a project already – I'll tell about it some other time. But I wasn't phoning about my future; it's the time beyond that I'm worrying about. What will you remember about me when I'm gone?'

Di hesitated for only an instant. 'You've always been a wonderful friend – you're fun, and you're caring, and you're always ready to listen to everyone's problems.'

If she'd been Joey, Alison would have purred.

'You do have a few foibles though; sometimes you verge on the eccentric...'

Alison's mood changed: 'What d'you mean?'

'Well...you must admit that punctuality isn't your strong point. If I arrive anywhere later than you then I know I'm really late! Didn't you turn up a day late for Phil's funeral service?'

Alison didn't need reminding of arriving at the empty church, driving to another one, then finally phoning the undertakers to hear that the funeral had been the previous day.

'But, Di, I'm not the only vague one. My friend Fiona went to a funeral the other day and halfway through she realised she was at the wrong grave... She could hardly leave at that point, so she stayed until this unknown person was buried, and then rushed across the cemetery and arrived just as everyone was leaving her aunt's graveside. Not nice.'

'But you *are* very forgetful,' Di warmed to the topic. 'You just need to be more organised. Do you ever use that transparent purse I gave you after you'd left your keys in the fridge? At least then you could see where they were. If only you'd put them in the same place every time!'

Di was showing her frustration now. 'It's a pity whistling keyrings went out of fashion. And it's not only keys; what about the cup of tea in the linen cupboard? And finding your ID book in the washing machine? And calling the electrician to fix the television set after that electric storm?'

'So I hadn't switched it on; not a major tragedy. I have an active mind.' Alison sounded huffy.

An expensive moment of active-mindedness. Joey was not impressed.

'I was hoping you'd find positive things to say,' Alison wailed. 'So what if I'm slightly scatty? You don't hear comments like that in funeral tributes. They're all about loving memories and interesting stories that make you feel sorry you didn't know the person better. What will you miss if I go?'

'Woah, look at the time! I've got to rush off now,' Di avoided the question. 'I'll think about it and let you know.'

Alison was left more depressed than before. Even her best friend couldn't find many positive points. That's *not* what friends are for...

'Thanks for nothing, Di. I think I'd better write my own obituary in advance.'

But that was definitely an ATM activity. Not even the thought of a cuppa could cheer her.

Heaven help us. Joey dropped her head onto her crossed paws.

But Alison put the kettle on anyway – and, of course, there was that last slice of apricot cake, from the other night when the temptation to bake had overcome the need to declutter. As she downed her coffee she felt the caffeine and the sugar working their magic. Enough self-pity. 'You'll feel better when you've *done* something,' she admonished herself. 'Get going on those photographs – now!'

She put on a CD that suited her mood: Beethoven's 5ᵗʰ Symphony. One surely couldn't get anything more persistent than that 'da-da-da-*dum*' first movement… That would do for a start.

No stopping her now! Several CDs later and she'd made amazing progress. Even Margie would be impressed. And Mandy would be so happy!

No comment from Joey. She'd long since retreated to the bedroom in the face of such frenetic activity.

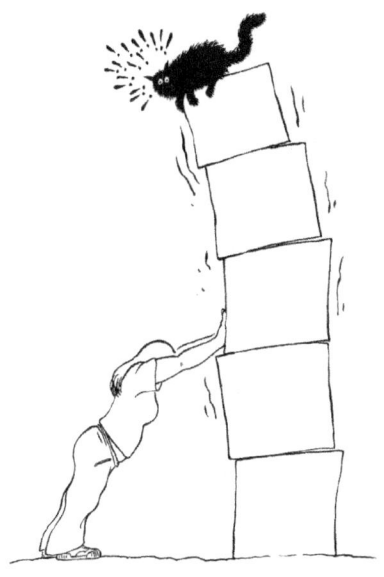

Hello, Dolly!

'Maybe yesterday's virtue will spill over to today,' Alison said to herself as she finished her breakfast cup of coffee. Today she'd deal with the bedroom cupboards (at least Mark's was empty). No photos – enough of those yesterday. And in any case she'd eventually got so much sorted: quite a big pile for Mandy, a smaller pile called 'Keep, not Mandy', and a really big pile all gone into the Out-box! Victory!

As she opened the bedroom cupboard, she caught sight of herself in the full-length mirror. 'Not great, but not too-oo bad,' she muttered aloud. 'I must be more serious about going to the gym. My tummy's still flabby. If it gets any worse, it'll look like Aunt Becky's Shar-Pei puppy… That's thanks to having two children at once…' Reality raised its head: 'But I've had decades to flatten it!'

She knew, though, that it was because of her inability to throw leftovers away… Now she had to throw parts of her life away.

She took one look at her clothes. 'Oh my goodness; there's no way I can sort this lot out on my own; I'll need some help. I'll phone Pam later. I'll do the bathroom now; that should be easy.'

Now that you're the expert. Joey followed her into the bathroom.

She opened a cupboard. Her heart sank…more shoeboxes. The first one was filled with samples that she'd gleaned from the make-up counters of various department stores. She'd really meant to use them – to take more care of her 'mature' (beautician-speak for aged/wrinkled/dried-up) skin. But there'd been no time in the morning rush to 'gently massage' her face with 'exotic plant oils' – barely time for soap and water (dirty words to the professional beautician) – and a dash of lipstick. Alison examined her face. 'Those aren't really wrinkles, they're laughter lines.' She raised her eyebrows soulfully.

Next box. Mascara, eye-liner, eyebrow pencils, eye-shadow and other 'essentials'. Without her glasses she couldn't see where to put eye makeup, so there was little point in keeping them. All she needed, surely, was two lipsticks: one at home, and one in the car for when she was really rushed? 'More decisions…must they really all go?'

Silly question.

Ignoring her cat, Alison picked out a plastic shower cap from the bottom of the make-up box and gathered her hair into it. She looked at herself in the mirror and giggled; she looked just like Andy Capp's wife! And whatever had happened to that fun bathing cap made of pink petals, with a long blonde plait? It must have perished – like their marriage…

'Don't go there,' she chided herself. 'Mark is gone and I can just about handle that.'

Back to the box. Oh yes, she'd been fashionable once. She even had the evidence! Where are those photos? No…that would mean revisiting her three piles – *not* a good idea. She sighed, remembering the bright green or blue eye-shadow, her heavily pencilled lids, the carefully drawn eyebrows (sometimes producing an unintentionally startled look), and the Joan Crawford eyelashes (like a row of steel armour – impractical if you were angling for a kiss).

She'd grow old without all these mod cons! Ta-da! Alison disposed of the lot. She was beginning to enjoy the destroying process. Hello, Margie!

She realised she was still wearing the shower cap. She pulled it off and shook her hair back into place. Hairdressers! Another tale! In her single days, Alison's Saturday mornings had been scheduled for the hairdresser. An Italian salon had been all the rage – André and Georgio, highly excitable and voluble, rushing about, bearing scissors and other relevant props, encouraged by the adoring clientele. Tea and sandwiches from a nearby restaurant sustained the captivated crowd.

Her most mortifying hair memory was in the 'bouffant' days. After a few hours of Lucia's teasing – tugging each hair almost from its roots – Alison was a Marge Simpson clone (not that there were any Simpsons in those days…). Too upset to comment, she'd dashed to the Ladies to brush out the cement-sprayed arrangement. Lucia entered, saw the destruction of her work of art, glowered and rushed out. *She* was annoyed? Being a non-confrontational person, Alison had had to change salons. She'd never understood why she, the paying victim, should have felt guilty when it was the hairdresser who had been at fault. Those days were over, and she was happy now with Raymond whom she visited when too much grey forced itself through the fading tint. Like now.

Alison thought back to her single days in the Sea Point flat with Kathy. Both of them had been far more concerned with their appearances in those days. She would never forget the 'Kathy wig saga' – a really 'bad hair day'. What on earth had Carlo been thinking? By the time Kathy had noticed what he was doing, it was too late. She'd been shorn; seriously shorn.

She threw a fit; there was no way she could teach looking like that. Distressed and de-tressed, she had reluctantly accepted Carlo's highly apologetic offer. He would provide her with a wig, at his own expense. However, this would take twenty-four hours as it had to be ordered from the suppliers, set and brushed into a Kathy-acceptable style. So she'd phoned in 'sick' and remained in the flat for two days until the wig arrived. All had been forgiven – but certainly not forgotten!

Joey licked her fur into a velvety sheen. *No new styles for her!*

Back to the cupboard. Out went the outdated hair accessories: clips, rollers, slides in the shape of butterflies (must be Mandy's, surely?), Alice bands, teasing combs. Next, the shampoos and shower caps and all sorts of goodies from decades of hotel stays with Mark. 'Well, they were there for our use,' she said defensively to Joey, who had stopped conditioning her coat in apparent shock.

Success breeds success! The medicine chest. Alison's interpretation of the Girl Guide's motto 'be prepared' had provided enough supplies for home use – and, if called upon, almost enough for the local pharmacy! She took a deep breath and spread everything on the bed. Bad mistake. Her duvet was now tinged with brown from a leaking iodine container... After sponging the damaged spot into a pink splodge she removed whatever had passed their sell-by date – she was beginning to take that phrase personally – into a paper bag. She'd offload them at the nearest pharmacy! Helping both herself and the environment! (Hello again, Margie!) She gazed at the half-empty shelves and congratulated herself. Was she becoming a declutter junkie?

Joey showed her teeth in a nervous smile.

Alison's glance fell on the remains of gift sets that she had kept for special occasions that hadn't yet arisen. Over the years popular fragrances had changed from flowers to fruit, and now to veggies! She could still smell her mother's 4711 and Yardley's English Rose and Lavender soaps and perfume. Only a qualified pharmacist could make sense of today's earthy, environmentally correct products. She'd just recently been accosted by a young, over-painted beautician who'd warned her that her skin would wither away without the instant use of the products 'for the more mature woman' that she was promoting. She'd finished off her patter of encouragement with: 'It even works for old ladies.' Another lost sale! What would she have said if she'd known that Alison's mother had relied on the soap that was used by '9 out of 10 film stars'! And what about the vanishing cream that her mother had used at night? Apparently when Alison was about three she'd wailed, 'Take it off, Mummy! I don't want you to vanish!'

Di's regular gift to herself was a back massage and foot treatment. Alison had enjoyed a facial on rare occasions such as the girls' weddings, but always had her eyes on her watch. So much else to do! She looked in the bathroom mirror. Perhaps it was time for another spa visit…

What next? The towels! There was no stopping her now. Alison placed all the towels on the now duvet-less bed and put aside those that had no partner – 'Like me,' she thought – and those that were worn out – ditto. She'd dreamed for decades of having complete sets of towels, and if not now, then when? She would be stylish in her flat! She hesitated momentarily about the hooded towels that had changed babies into snug cuddle-bunnies, but resolutely ('Be strong, Ally') added them to the Out pile! The grandchildren were no longer babies and the nearby orphanage would welcome them. The children's blankets expertly crocheted by her mum? Those would go too! Mum would be happy that others were now enjoying her handiwork.

A quick coffee break, and she was back on the job. Joey blinked.

Okay, now for the linen cupboard. Peeking out from the bottom of the pile were the colourfully hand-embroidered table-cloths, one red, one black, that they'd bought on honeymoon in Lourenço Marques. She'd seldom used them, keeping them only for special occasions. As children they'd had everyday and 'special occasion' clothes, food and treats – and the habit had permeated into Alison's adult life. Would the girls take them? She could already hear the cries of 'Who'll wash them, and iron them?' Plastic or drip-dry cloths, and individual place mats for this century – much more practical, thanks, Ma. Now this? Oh! This one, also hand-embroidered, she'd made herself – well, almost. Those endless hours embroidering cross-stitch squares… Alison had found the repetition deeply boring and had gratefully handed the squares over to her mother to join together with the compulsory heavy ecru lace. And now here it was, nearly half a century later, a still-attractive tablecloth! She'd keep these three; the rest could go.

Sheets! Those hideous floral sheets! Novel and colourful when she'd been given them for her trousseau. They were good quality, and nowhere near worn out. She could give them away… Then she could replace them with the new range she'd seen in the shops, beautiful soft percale, white and beige. She cheered up – she'd splash out on a new set – or two – and a duvet – the works!

Inspired by the successful cleansing operation, Alison turned to the kitchen. How many spice containers did one need? She ditched several almost empty ones without a thought – practice makes perfect! She'd read somewhere that their life-span was six months, which meant that most of them were on their way out, along with several small bottles of originally-green herbs, now a scentless grey. She'd grow her own in the new flat. No need to throw out then!

Almost drunk with success, she attacked the grocery cupboard, piling the entire contents onto the kitchen table. She groaned at the half-empty tins of solidified coffee and cocoa, and the unopened, seriously out-of-date containers of exotic foods. Whatever had she been thinking? Too much recipe reading! She'd enthusiastically tick recipes that appealed to her, buy the ingredients, then wait for that special occasion. Or just forget that she even had them. What a waste… Into the bin! To be joined almost immediately by half a dozen equally outdated jars and bottles – unwanted presents. 'Join your fellow castaways!' she declaimed.

Some packets were worth taking, though. Alison gathered the array of pasta containers, filled with varying amounts of… spaghetti, spaghettini, lasagne, tagliatelle, linguini, fusilli, penne, macaroni… Pasta was the peak of her cooking-for-one efforts – inspired by memories of the many unforgettable meals she'd relished on that first-ever Italian holiday, when she was twenty-four. Before Mark. She managed to fit them all into a zip-top supermarket bag. ATM, she'd decant the pasta into her new grocery cupboard. At least she'd have something to eat on arrival.

Alison looked triumphantly at the bulging rubbish bin. She felt so much better. Margie was right! It really was a cathartic experience. Why hadn't Margie phoned today? Just when wanted to boast about her extraordinary successes.

On to the cupboard filled with salad bowls and platters, from stainless steel to the huge white china ones. She placed them on the table and ruthlessly set aside the large ones that she wouldn't need in her new life. The enormous punchbowl and its dozen glasses – 'they'll none of them be missed'. She'd offer them to Gina and Gemma and then the charity shops.

Over the years she and Mark had collected a variety of drinking glasses for all occasions – from crystal tumblers (too good to use) to Irish whiskey glasses embossed with green shamrocks (too ugly to use). She'd keep a few wine glasses and the rest could go! And the decanters – strange that Mark hadn't taken them, after collecting them so assiduously… Out with them! And the vases from the next shelf – all except two of them could go! (Thank heavens for charity shops…)

Should she leave the drawers full of gadgets for another day? She was a salesman's dream: no matter how improbable the claims, she just had to buy. Television ads offering '…but that's not all…' sent her rushing to the shops. She, who initially hadn't known what to do with the most basic culinary tools, couldn't resist gadgets designed for professional caterers: 'no tears' onion choppers, and veggie slicers that cut the food – and one's fingers – into unusual shapes. And of course the plastic fruit squeezer that had seemed so useful in the demo when she'd gone with Jen to the Ideal Kitchens exhibition all those years ago. Jen, that paragon of tidiness, was never tempted by new-fangled gadgets; she had just a few necessary, basic items that worked, and *her* kitchen drawers opened and closed quite easily... 'Just you wait, Jen! My new flat will be perfect!'

At the back of a kitchen drawer she found a plastic bag filled with booklets explaining how to use her appliances, some of which, she noted, had been thrown out years before. Oh for a simple appliance with just one switch – On and Off, for people like her. One booklet even came with a CD! Imagine playing a CD to find out how to use your iron! She bundled them all back into the plastic bag. Not now, later. And the other drawers could wait till much later.

Joey continued to snore...

Alison looked at the bulging bags, boxes and empty cupboard spaces with pride. Time for a toast! She filled a wine glass with her 'special occasion' sparkling wine: 'To Me!' She really had achieved something! She put down her glass (one of the few she'd be taking to the flat) and spun round the room: 'I am the declutt'ring queen!' she sang à la Meryl Streep in *Mamma Mia!* Though where was her Pierce Brosnan?

Joey scrunched up her eyes as if in pain. *It had been a pleasant catnap until now...*

My Hometown

Alison replaced the receiver slowly. Bad news: Margie was coming to help her... She looked helplessly at Joey, who rolled her eyes and glided silently towards the door.

'Don't you dare leave me,' she threatened. 'Fraidy cat!'

She opened the fridge door. Thank goodness there was enough there to concoct a healthy salad, and somewhere at the back of the grocery cupboard there should be a packet of rooibos tea that she kept for health-conscious friends. Should she dash to the corner bakery for some rye bread, and maybe something decadent for tea? She'd need extra strength...

No, that would have to wait. The decluttering must go on,

especially since she was on such a roll! Where to start today? Margie's impending presence reminded her that there was still a shoebox of photos, labelled 'Holidays'. How efficient! Had *she* done that? A brief peep showed, however, that they were in no particular order – just tons of black and white snaps, dating from their own childhood holidays at Inchanga and Ceres, to coloured photos from later holidays in the 'Berg with Mark and the twins, and, most recently, Cape Town with Mark…

She looked into the box again. 'There must be enough childhood memories to share with Margie. Surely we can enjoy those together? I can leave sorting them till she gets here. As long as she doesn't try to make me throw them out…'

Alison looked at her watch. 'Heavens! Margie will be on her way already, and look at the mess!'

After a superficial tidying of the house, Alison grabbed her car keys – unusually in their right place at the front door – and dashed out to do the shopping before her sister's arrival.

She returned home with far more than she'd intended buying, but *she* couldn't live on rabbit food alone! Certainly not under the stress she was about to undergo! She unpacked her favourite butternut soup, some fresh fruit and, defiantly, a delicious-looking carrot cake for morning tea. Carrots are healthy, aren't they? But with cream cheese icing…?

Alison looked at her watch. Just enough time to put the salad together for later, and dolly it up with blue cheese and crushed peanut brittle. No time for caramelising nuts. She'd eat it even if Margie wouldn't.

Margie breezed in enthusiastically, carrying a basket of home-grown veggies, herbs, sprouts and a lentil pie – 'to help us along'. But now it was time for tea…

Margie made no comment about the carrot cake, except to say that she had a really good recipe of her own. But she managed to demolish two slices, along with her rooibos tea. Things were looking up. Alison smiled with relief.

'Right,' said Margie in her major-general voice as she opened the box of holiday photos, 'No time to waste!' She picked up the first photo. Her voice softened. 'Ah, Ceres... Heaven on earth... It was "our" place long before it became the home of fruit juice.'

'Did you also write about Ceres at school when we had to write compositions about "My Home Town"?' asked Alison.

'Of course not; my home town was Maritzburg.'

'Tch. No wonder you became a bookkeeper! It's much more fun being imaginative!'

'At least I was honest.'

'I bet Miss Thatcher didn't mind reading about Ceres. What a relief to read about some place other than Sleepy Hollow!'

Margie shrugged her shoulders.

Alison looked at the photograph again. 'I loved Ceres...I loved being part of such a large family. Bill and Jeremy were like our older brothers, and Zoë was like a sister my own age... Oh, and that boisterous boxer – Rex! It was like living inside our own Enid Blyton story: *Five Cousins and a Dog*.'

'You always lived in a world of books,' laughed Margie.

'What was so special about those holidays?' Alison wondered aloud. 'The cousins, of course. But lots more than that. What do you specially remember?'

'Sleeping on the stoep; we all loved that.'

'And waking up to fresh figs that Aunt Ann had picked early that morning.'

'Yes, and berries straight from the garden!' enthused Margie.

'With real thick cream from the farm.'

Cream? Joey cocked an ear.

'And when Aunt Ann let us pick flowers for the house...'

'You certainly inherited her love of gardening, Margie.'

'Yes, but you also enjoyed cutting those flowers...'

Alison nodded. 'I can still see that tin bath standing on the old wooden table on the stoep, filled with newly picked roses – all colours... And their perfume...' She breathed in ecstatically. 'Then Aunt Ann would fill the house with the roses – in jugs, vases, even her bowling trophies – whatever she could find... Do you remember?'

'Of course I remember! And the fragrance from the lilac tree at the front gate... But come on, let's get back to work.'

'Here's a picture of Rex!' Alison exclaimed. '*Without* one of the neighbour's chickens in his mouth!'

'Oh yes! He did keep catching them, didn't he? It was quite embarrassing. And Aunt Ann was forever having to buy live chickens to replace them!'

'Rex must have been so confused,' said Alison, 'when he brought chickens home he got into trouble. But remember that Oom Muller – with his freshly caught trout? Bringing fresh fish was acceptable; bringing newly killed chicken was not!'

'And Aunt Ann dreaded deboning the trout!' Margie reminded Alison. 'He always stayed to eat them, so she couldn't even give them away!'

Give away fish? Why wasn't I there?

'Remember how we couldn't control our giggling at lunch when the boys licked their lips and made facetious comments about how delicious it was?' Alison giggled again at the thought.

'And you ran out of the room choking. But it was from laughter, not bones! Poor Oom; he was so worried!

They sat silent for a while, each busy with her memories. Margie – naturally – was the first to come down to earth.

'Let's divide the photos into those you can throw away and the few that you'll keep.'

However, even with Margie's help, the Keep pile soon outgrew the Out pile. And distractions were many.

'Ah! Look at this, Margie! It's the swimming pool in the pine forest! We were all trying to balance on a tractor tyre. Remember? Seconds later it capsized and we all landed in the water! We should have had a video of that!'

'There can't be a more beautiful setting...the pine forest, the mountains and the river that literally runs through the pool!' Even Margie was getting carried away.

'Mom hired bicycles for us and we'd all cycle there. Except over Lover's Bridge – do you remember how scared we were when we had to walk across on those wooden planks? I was terrified that one of them would break and I'd go hurtling into the water, bike and all.'

'Hmm, yes; it *was* a high bridge – at least it seemed high to us then,' agreed Margie.

'And on the way home we'd crack the *dennepitte* out of the pinecones! The ones the squirrels hadn't got to...'

'Yes, and remember how we loved splashing in the 'sloots'! It was so special; we didn't have permanently running water next to the pavement in Maritzburg!'

'But Mum wasn't all that impressed with our wet clothes!' Alison reminded her.

'Yes, and how we used to go at 8 o'clock at night – just us kids, with Rex for protection – to Luyt's Tea Room to wait for the Pullman from Cape Town to arrive with the *Cape Argus* newspaper. That was a true adventure for us city cousins!'

Alison laughed, 'I think Rex came with us more for his regular walk than for our protection!'

'And after collecting the paper, we'd go on to the tea garden for ice cream cones.'

'Peppermint!'

'Chocolate!' Margie was a teenager again.

'Yes, but you must admit that for you the main attraction wasn't the ice cream; it was that Japie de Beer, who worked there at night!'

Margie chuckled. 'Unrequited love, from the other side of the counter!'

'I wasn't interested in boys; I just wanted books,' said Alison. 'Do you remember how once a week we'd walk over to the library. It was open at night – quite strange really. That's where I became addicted to the *Maasdorp* school series. The children in those books had such fun – midnight feasts and picnic hampers... And by the way,' she laughed, 'do you see how many of my memories involve food? For me, nothing has changed. Not like you; you've become so health conscious...'

'Well, organic gardening makes sense and works for me.' Margie sounded quite defensive.

'And Peter and Graham?'

'Oh yes, of course! Peter goes along with my ideas.'

'Not really,' thought Alison. 'He's too docile a husband to look for trouble...'

'And Graham's very conscious of eating the right food,' Margie continued.

Alison smiled to herself, remembering how her nephew relished her comfort food when Margie was out of the way. 'Don't you ever crave something decadent?'

'Not really,' Margie admitted. 'It's a way of life; a matter of discipline.'

'Hmm; and that's where I lose out,' Alison thought.

Then Margie added: 'But I do occasionally break out for something like that carrot cake. It was so more-ish!'

Alison chuckled. 'She's becoming human,' she thought with amusement.

They worked steadily through the boxes, quietly re-living their childhood – and adding to the 'Keep' pile, Alison noted happily.

Margie's cellphone rang. It was Peter: 'Where are you? I've forgotten what time you told me to put the stove on.'

Alison shook her head, 'How on earth did we manage without cellphones?'

Margie laughed. 'Remember the wind-up phone at Aunt Ann's house? If she didn't answer the operator would say, "There's no reply. Shall I try Mrs Miller's number? She's probably there".'

'It was just like that old soapie *Nommer Asseblief*, with the operator knowing everyone's business! And you had to book a trunk call in advance. No wonder the kids today can't relate to the "olden days". They probably don't even know what a trunk call is! *Was*, I should say.' Another topic for Mandy's project. Mental note: 'Tell her that a long-distance call was called a "trunk call".'

Alison looked at the ever-growing Keep pile. 'Admit defeat, Margie! Let my photos go!' she sang.

'Well, as long as you have space for them. You can ask Graham to show you how to burn them onto a CD.' Margie was happy to offer her son's services.

An unexpected reprieve! Alison looked at her watch. Lunch!

Alison was relieved and pleased that Margie enjoyed her culinary contributions, and Alison had to admit that the lentil pie and health offerings were really tasty.

The reminiscences continued during lunch.

'Aunt Ann's garden! Those berries we used to steal, remember, Margie? I'm sure Aunt Ann turned a blind eye, especially since they left telltale purple and red stains on our hands and feet... And the overloaded peach and plum trees... and the pergola loaded with juicy grapes...'

'The village certainly lived up to its namesake, the Goddess of Fruitfulness!' laughed Margie.

Fruit? Joey didn't quite see the point.

'It was so different from city life,' said Alison, 'even in those days. In Ceres the children rode bicycles or walked; in Maritzburg we mostly went in double-decker buses. And Maritzburg people used to complain about the trip to Durban – but the people from Ceres happily drove for three hours over two mountain passes to get to Cape Town!'

'Yes, and front doors were left open or unlocked! Remember how Aunt Ann used to scold Mum for locking the doors at night? "You're not in Maritzburg now!" she'd say.'

Margie, Ally and Zoë slept on the stoep that surrounded the house. Alison never admitted it, but she was secretly scared of sleeping outside, although she loved looking at the stars that shone so brightly in the unpolluted air. Jeremy had added to her fears with stories about shooting stars that fell onto houses! For years afterwards she'd ducked her head when she'd thought she saw a shooting star! So unlike the brave Secret Seven children!

'And the pantry!' Alison warmed to her subject. 'That enticing pantry – separated from the kitchen by a green mesh door. I so remember those shelves of bottled fruit, and jams, and berry syrups and – oh yes! – ginger beer in those stone bottles with special wire thingies at the top to keep the fizz in! It was like a nursery rhyme picture book come to life!'

'There you go, living in books again,' said Margie.

They took their empty plates to the kitchen. 'Thanks, I really enjoyed that,' said Margie. 'What shall we do next?'

'There's something I can't do alone. I'm so pleased you're here. I found Dad's tin box among the photos.'

Margie couldn't have come at a better time. Alison really needed her sister to be with her for this. The tin box lay at the back of the cupboard; she could hardly bring herself to touch it. There was no way she could have done it on her own.

They gazed at the small tin box. 'That's all he left of himself,' Alison murmured. 'His whole life stored in this one old box.'

'We were absolutely forbidden to open it,' recalled Margie. 'The only time I remember Dad being angry with us was when he found us looking inside it when the cousins were visiting and Bill dared us to open it. Dad snatched it from Jeremy's hands and chased us all out of the room. It had a few photos, and letters, mostly in Russian or Yiddish, and some documents. He couldn't bear to even let us see them.'

'Those memories were just too painful for him,' said Alison. 'Even Mum was never allowed to look inside the box. But I think she understood…'

'Go on, open it,' urged Margie.

'No, you do it. You're the eldest.'

Margie took a deep breath, opened the box and gazed at the sparse contents. 'I feel guilty doing this now that Dad's gone,' she muttered. 'These photos are in good condition. Do you think we can find some family resemblances?'

They laid the pictures out carefully – babies in prams, smiling young couples, and a dignified older generation. Who were they, and at what family gatherings had the pictures been taken?

Alison picked up a photograph that had fallen onto the floor. 'Look at this one, Margie. The children look so solemn and soulful. Those clothes must have been dreadfully uncomfy and restricting... I wonder why they had this obsession with sailor suits?'

Margie smiled in agreement. 'Those were certainly not child-centred days. Mind you, are today's mothers so different – dressing their babies in impractical denim dungarees?'

'Yes, and little denim caps and hats instead of bonnets...'

Alison placed the photograph next to the others 'It's so sad that we don't know who these people are,' she said. 'They must be Dad's family – *our* family. If only he'd written their names on the back.'

'And he never heard from most of them after he fled from Lithuania. He was only sixteen... Imagine carrying memories of your beloved family and keeping them for seventy years, not knowing what had happened to them...' Margie's voice broke a little.

'The only time he mentioned his family was during those last few days before he died, when he was drifting in and out of consciousness,' said Alison. 'There was that day when he lifted his head from the pillows and announced: "My brother is coming to stay. I haven't seen him for so long." Then he asked me to "please make him a nice supper". I just had to play along, so I said "Of course, Dad, I'll make baked fish." "Good," he said, "he likes fish." Then he sank back onto the pillow, with a satisfied smile on his face. Then a moment later he started again: "We used to go fishing together then our mother would bake the catch when we got home. In winter we had to crack the ice in the river to get to the fish!" Then he smiled again and wafted back to his own world.' Alison had tears in her eyes.

They browsed through the written contents.

Margie broke the silence: 'It's like reading history—'

'That's exactly what it is,' interrupted Alison, 'It *is* our family history.'

'This one's in Yiddish; I can't read it. Oh but here's one in German. Wait; let me figure it out. It's from a friend of his brother Max, begging Dad to try harder to get him to South

Africa. Listen to what he says: "Max is very sick and must leave here. He is too weak to write himself. The pogroms have hit the villages near here and it won't be long before we are attacked. We are all making plans to get away, anywhere, we will not survive here... I am going to America to cousins in New York. I pray we will all meet when these terrible times are over." That's it.' Margie wiped her eyes.

'No wonder he couldn't bear to re-live those horrors. The worst thing is that he tried so hard to save Max, and all in vain. Imagine living with that all these years...'

'Well, we just have to believe that they are all reunited now...'

'Close the box,' said Alison, 'and let's just remember them – the family we never knew.'

O Sole Mio

This was tiring work! Alison poured her coffee, made a tuna mayo sandwich and sat down in front of the television to enjoy the latest scandals in *Isidingo*…

'Well, I deserve it, don't I? Margie said so,' she justified herself to the supercilious cat.

She'd have an early night, enjoy her new Donna Leon book, and be up with the chirping sparrows to continue the sorting process.

The phone rang again. She answered with assurance. She'd spoken to Margie earlier to update her on the work-in-progress. 'Pam! Tonight? Should I? I was going to have an early night.'

'Come on, when was the last time you saw a live Italian opera in Durban? And it's *La Bohème*...'

'Oh! Why not? Sure, I'll be ready.'

When had this obsession with opera started? They'd been brought up on Gilbert and Sullivan, the cultural highlight of the Maritzburg Royal Show week! Mum had played the violin in the orchestra and she and Margie went to every dress rehearsal and matinee. Alison's dream of taking part in an operetta became a reality when she arrived in Cape Town to study music. All singing students were expected to take part in the UCT opera chorus. She'd chosen singing because she thought it was an easy option! No lugging heavy instruments and having to tune them.

The thrill of being part of a professional full-scale opera! Though she had to admit that it lost some of the magic from the other side of the curtain. Instead of that tingling moment when Tosca flings herself over the wall of the Castel Sant'Angelo, Alison now knew that she landed on a mattress! And the unforgettable night when Lorna, in *Il Seraglio*, blacked out her teeth, explaining that she was the elderly 'madam' of the harem.

Armed with little beyond the producer's constant direction to the chorus 'Do notta stand een a straighta line,' Alison produced her first school operetta at Carlton Junior. It wasn't all smooth running; she'd had tears initially from Charlie, a rugby-playing youngster who was cast as a girl – who could blame him! The venue was an old church hall, with limited stage access, and Charlie had to be shoved, petticoats and all, through a tiny window to get onto the stage. The piano accompanist – no keyboard or guitar band – sitting at her piano in an alcove off-stage, had to shine a torch to let the cast know when she was ready to begin the overture. The backdrop was a roll-up canvas blind, painted by the pregnant art teacher, balancing precariously on a ladder. After much pleading to the headmaster about the lack of stage lighting, Alison had grudgingly been given one fixed spot, centre-stage! It was a very basic production, but clearly successful and enormous fun. And she'd learnt a huge amount!

Years later she'd gazed in awe at the new state-of-the art school theatre. She could just hear Miffie's reaction: '*My magtig!*' 'Amazing facilities, but we were the pioneers,' she thought with pride.

Mr Walker, the headmaster at Carlton, was a moody man. Each morning, before choosing the hymn of the day Alison would check with his long-suffering secretary as to the 'weather conditions'. If his mood was merely 'cloudy' she'd choose *All Things Bright and Beautiful* – and sometimes he'd react with a cynical smile. If conditions were thunderous, she'd warn the staff with *O God, Our Help in Ages Past*. She was a musical meteorologist!

Mr Lawson, the headmaster of her next school, Glenby High, was also a musician. Most of his staff were musical. Whenever there was a position vacant – sport, woodwork, science – the advertisement in the *Government Gazette* would contain the words: 'Interest in music an advantage'. One season the local Gilbert and Sullivan Society production included five of the Glenby staff!

Alison was one of the piano accompanists for *Trial by Jury*, and invited Miss Edwards, who had retired to Cape Town, to the opening night; Eddie was delighted at the thought of seeing her former pupil perform. After she'd settled Eddie in the front row, Alison joined the rest of orchestra in the pit. She was about to sit down, when Fred, the co-accompanist whispered, 'I hope you've brought the keys.' Alison's mind went blank. She'd been given the keys of the hired pianos and had absolutely no idea where they were! She furtively tried every available key from house to car keys while the management hovered threateningly: 'If you damage the pianos it will be your responsibility.' Almost in tears, she rushed to the public phone. Her flatmate, Kathy, who happened to be home, eventually found the keys, and spluttered to the theatre in her ancient Volksie. Relief knew no bounds.

Eddie said afterwards that she'd thoroughly enjoyed the performance, but what a pity it had started so late...

'Oh, that's show business for you,' Alison had replied airily. But she was not surprised when she wasn't invited to accompany the following season...

Loud hooting interrupted Alison's wanderings. Pam here already! 'Come inside; I won't be long!' Joey shook her head in shame.

They made it to the theatre in time. As always, the tragic plot and the evocative music moved her deeply. Unwelcome thoughts of her own situation made matters worse. 'Any more tissues?' she asked Pam tearfully as the final curtain fell.

They made their way to the nearest coffee shop. Some members of the orchestra were at the next table: 'Were we so bad we made you cry?' they teased.

'No-o, it was just so beautiful,' Alison sniffed.

Coffee was extended to a much-needed supper and chat. By the time the meal had ended, Alison was feeling more cheerful. Not for long though.

'How's the packing going?' Pam's question brought her back to reality.

'Don't ask! I haven't even *got* to the packing stage; I'm still sorting out what I can take and what I need to get rid of... Margie doesn't approve of my dismal organisational skills; she phones every day to check on my progress. You know me, Pam, I'm useless at making decisions, especially about change – and there's so much to decide about in such a short time. How did I collect so much unnecessary clutter? I should have cleared things out every year. But it's the memories attached to the things that make it so difficult. Every time I open a cupboard I find something that takes me back; I'm spending hours just thinking of the past...'

'Can't you make a schedule – and force yourself to stick to it?'

'Oh, Pam, you have no idea of what it's like; unless you've gone through it yourself you can't really understand. I feel everyone's so critical of me – even Joey.'

'Joey?' Pam looked at her anxiously.

'Yes: Joey, Don't look at me like that; I'm not losing it!'

Pam wasn't going to argue. 'How about some more coffee?'

On the way home they spoke of operas they'd seen and taken part in. Alison's mood lightened.

'Good night, Pam, and thank you. That was just what I needed – Mimi's problems put mine into perspective. I feel so much better now.'

Yet once inside the house Alison felt strangely unsettled. She was stimulated by the echoes of Puccini's glorious music that went round in her head, and at the same time she felt depressed by her lack of progress in the moving preparations.

Despite having planned an early, relaxing night she now felt guilty about having gone to the opera when she could have done more clearing. She was wide awake and decided that she might as well do something worthwhile. She'd tackle the postcards from her first trip to the land of opera! She eventually found the box, under a stack of photo albums, and took it through to her bedroom. Yes! This was what she'd been hoping for – the cards and memorabilia from that first crazy holiday abroad – in Italy! Alitalia air ticket, bus tickets, even sweet-wrappings and, of course, restaurant receipts. And so many postcards…

Who sends postcards in these days of email and Skype and Twitter? Not with the price of the cards and postage. Such a pity; cellphones might be quicker and more efficient, but they lack the romance and excitement of a postcard with stamps from afar! She stopped. 'Remembering when' was her constant topic. Blame it on the move…

Italy! She was passionate about the people, the food, and especially the music. 'Why?' she wondered. Had she been Italian in a previous life?

The fascination had begun at university. The Marcello Mastroianni look-alike lecturer, who, although reputedly a Casanova, had treated her with the kindness reserved for his more naïve students. She'd read eagerly about Italian life and enrolled at the Berlitz language school. She and her teacher, Bianca, met regularly for lunch at a Sea Point trattoria and she gradually progressed from shyly greeting the owners to discussing the menu with them – minestrone, focaccia, ravioli… Such a musical language! Firenze, Venezia, Milano – so much more appealing and romantic than the English translations. She'd appreciated Jamie Oliver's story of his missing the turn-off to Florence as he was looking for the Florence sign!

She picked up a postcard of the leaning tower of Pisa and chuckled. It reminded her of Gemma and Gina's introduction to the language when they went to Italy on holiday after their graduation. On arrival in a little Tuscan village, Gemma had guarded the luggage at the station while her sister searched for accommodation. She returned chuffed with success and asked the taxi-driver to drive them to 'the Albergo'. The more he questioned 'What *albergo*?', the more she desperately explained: 'The one with the Albergo sign. That's the one we want.' It was minutes before the penny dropped and they realised that *albergo* just meant 'hotel'.

Here was a small, matt postcard of the Duomo in Milan, lit up and looking like an elaborately iced cake. The card couldn't do justice to the extravagant architecture, but it reminded Alison of why she'd bought it. The taxi driver had screeched past the church before she could take a photo. In her handbag was the ticket she'd bought back in Durban for *La Bohème* at La Scala – she wasn't travelling six thousand miles to find that the opera season was fully booked!

Her first sight of the opera house had been a disappointment. The bus driver announced in operatic tones, 'La Scala!' She looked around. Had she heard incorrectly? Where was the famous opera house? Summoning up her courage and her best Italian she asked a young man, '*Dov'e La Scala?*' He pointed at a dowdy mustard-coloured building. She repeated the question with more precise diction. With obvious amusement he pointed again at the building, and replied in perfect English.

'It doesn't look like the Paris Opera House from the outside, but inside: "Mmmwa!"' – he kissed his fingers with an Italian flourish!

She gazed at the opera advertisements pasted around the building. The most prestigious opera house in the world! She knew that one shouldn't always judge a building from the outside – well, this was the living proof of that. And where were the queues of opera lovers? It was at that moment that she'd added a new and unwelcome word to her vocabulary – *il sciopero* – the strike! 'The red line through the advertisement means "Performance cancelled",' the young man explained.

'Why now?'

'The World Trade Fair! The city is overflowing with business people from all over the world! What better time for the opera staff to strike?'

An expensive way to learn a new word, she thought miserably.

Sensing her unhappiness, Luigi, having introduced himself, explained that the trattorias were definitely not on strike! Would she perhaps join him for coffee? He was not as entertaining as the opera, but he'd try! To her surprise she accepted the invitation and they had spent an entertaining evening chatting in reasonable Italian! She'd asked him where he'd learnt such excellent English – he'd worked for two years as a bellhop at a London hotel. He was no playboy – maybe she was too homely – and he'd returned her to the *pensione*, gallantly adding that for him the *sciopero* had been a lucky strike!

The next postcard? Venezia! Rising magically from the sea, the brightly coloured palazzos, every centimetre a theatrical set. Mundane conversation spoken with extravagant gestures and in lyrical tones.

Would she ever forget Venice and her visit to Murano? She didn't need the vase to remind her. She'd joined a group on the Piazza San Marco. There appeared to be some excitement; everyone was talking at once. She recognised the dreaded word *sciopero* again!

'The water transport!'

'In the city of islands?'

'Impossible!'

General confusion all around.

Alison's group moved across to the centre of the piazza where a small crowd was gathering around an actor in fancy-dress costume, who was declaiming excitedly. Were they shooting a film? Not at all. The 'actor' was a municipal manager in full regalia, announcing to the crowd of eager tourists that free transport was leaving immediately for Murano! He gabbled on while Alison, delighted with her Italian expertise, boarded the waiting *vaporetto*.

On the island, she first enjoyed a delicious pizza – the dough thin and the topping generous. Fortified, she wandered around the canals and palazzos – houses rather than palaces – enjoying the atmosphere. Later on she'd bought her treasured red vase from one of the many little curio shops.

Venice was beckoning her back across the sea. But suddenly the island seemed strangely free of tourists and the sea free of boats... *Sciopero* was the only word that she recognised from the pitying answers to her questions. There must be a way back! She ran in vain from one vaporetto stop to the next. Where was everyone? She couldn't spend the night here. She was expected back at the *pensione* and still had so much to explore in Venice...

In the distance she saw a motorboat approaching. As it raced past her she read the word 'Polizia'. A police *vaporetto*? She shouted and waved frantically until the roar of the engine changed tone and the boat turned back – and stopped right in front of her. As she boarded it joyfully, she imagined the caption on a photograph in the *Natal Mercury*: 'Police escort for Durban teacher'. One of the policemen, charming, and amused at her predicament, asked if she had forgotten that the last *vaporetto* had returned an hour earlier. She'd missed that part of the announcement as she'd hurried aboard, proud that she had understood the municipal manager's announcement before the other tourists.

The remaining days reminded her of the film *If It's Tuesday,*

This Must Be Belgium – a ridiculous rush to absorb as much as possible of this beautiful country in the remaining few days.

When her holiday finally came to an end, she'd collapsed onto the plane, waking just in time for breakfast before it landed at Jan Smuts Airport. She'd phoned home from there to remind her parents of her arrival time in Durban. Her father had been surprised to hear her voice.

No, they hadn't received a postcard with her flight details! Hadn't there been a postal strike in Italy?

Alison returned the postcards to their box and tipped everything else into the waste-paper bin. She felt less guilty now that she'd achieved something – a good ending to the evening. She yawned. Perhaps just time for a *biscotto*?

Perfetto!

Over the Rainbow

Alison awoke to the cheery sound of birdsong, and through the window she saw sparrows dancing the twist after a dip in the birdbath. She'd miss them, she thought, but the sun would rise again and other birds would sing outside the new flat. Not an early bird herself, she sat on the stoep to watch the sunrise. Inspired, she decided she'd start the day early too.

Instead of the usual gulped-down tea or coffee, she'd fortify herself with a real breakfast: scrambled eggs (eggs now off the danger list and apparently good for you – until the next time), tomato and brown toast. Please note, Margie: brown bread, sometimes rye! When she was a child eggs were an essential part of the daily breakfast. As was butter! Wasn't it 'really better with real butter'? Milk from bottles, delivered by a real live milkman. Margie was always first to prise off the cardboard lid, and eat the cream that had settled at the top! Later on the caps were made of foil, festive red ones with embossed sprigs of holly at Christmas time!

She'd lived through so many changes, not only in her personal life. Aunt Ann had made cream cheese by pouring and sifting milk through a muslin bag – the genuine article, without the list of chemical additives found on present-day tubs. What a mission, trying to decipher the ingredients of ordinary foods... Not worth the effort. Fads were in today, out tomorrow... Her mother had taken two heaped teaspoons of sugar in every cup of tea, and she'd lived until eighty-seven! 'When life is tough you make it easier,' she'd philosophised. Alison had been delighted to read that the latest studies had shown that a piece of dark chocolate every night is good for the heart!

So she'd had her sustenance for today's programme. Her own 'To Do' list (Margie's organisational skills were catching!), in bold red koki, commanded: Clothes!

Clothes, oh no... She couldn't avoid them any longer. Or perhaps she could... She looked around the study for an alternative. The children's books! Brilliant idea! Back to the days when children were children... She'd shelve the clothes for now – no pun intended – and concentrate on books. What a relief.

What a surprise... Joey sighed.

Before she could change her mind, Alison went into the spare room and began removing books from the shelf and putting them onto the bed.

The bookshelves were really dusty. 'I'd better clean them first,' she thought. In the kitchen she opened the cupboard under the sink and realised that it was filled with unlovely objects due for the dustbin: empty or half-empty containers of kitchen cleaners and detergents, and lots of grubby well-used dusters and stained cleaning brushes... Useless, she thought. Where were the *clean* dusters? Should she replace them all before she moved? Do it now! She grabbed her handbag, found the car keys, then stopped at the door. 'No, you're just procrastinating,' she scolded herself. 'Get on with it; use the dusters that are here.' She returned to the bedroom, dusters in hand.

Her family had inherited her love of books. She'd been thrilled the day Mandy had said to her, 'When we were small you read us *Ameliaranne and the Green Umbrella*, Granny. Now I can read it myself! And I found some more Ameliaranne stories at the library. What else do you think I should read, Granny?'

Alison picked up *Little Grey Rabbit's Birthday* – her very own copy, not one of Margie's hand-me-downs – a prize given to each child at the end of Standard 1. She had been so proud that she and the author, Alison Uttley, shared first names! Perhaps that was where she'd got her fascination with names. She'd treasured the book, whose creatures had become her friends. 'There's no way I'm giving my friends away,' she said to herself.

The Beatrix Potter books, posters and records had soon become part of the twins' childhood, and they had in turn passed their fascination on to their own children. Those catchy songs and beautifully spoken stories... Alison panicked: where were they? Disregarding Margie's rules, she dived into the full Out-box and rescued some of the children's LPs. 'Some clutter is necessary; life is not only about the future,' she philosophised to a rather scornful-looking Joey.

Margie and Alison had enrolled as members of the public library when Alison was very young. On Saturdays they would catch the bus to town with their mother, exchange the week's books at the library, and hurry to the tiny kiosk in Theatre Lane where Alison would buy the latest Enid Blyton *Sunny Stories*. Could they have cost only sixpence each? How she'd loved sharing in life at Green Hedges! She'd entered every competition and, as proof, here on the top shelf was a dusty copy of the *Enid Blyton Omnibus* she'd won in a *Sunny Stories* competition! Probably an antique, she giggled, noting the year and re-reading the inscription by the author herself!

Alison had recently bought Enid Blyton's biography, which told of a life very different from the stories she'd written. Alison Uttley had despised Enid Blyton's books, but Margie and Ally had loved them all: from the Faraway Tree and Mr Pink-whistle to the Famous Five, the Secret Seven and the Malory Towers series. Alison was delighted when Enid Blyton had come back into favour after years of being banned by the political-correctness police. 'And now they're available on Kindle!' she thought happily, as she put the omnibus into the In-box, 'Who says reading is dying out?'

On those Saturday mornings, after Alison had bought her *Sunny Stories*, and Margie her *School Friend*, they'd go with their mother to Christies – it had an upstairs! – or to the more sedate Kean's Tea Room. Their mother would sometimes meet her friends there during the week – tea and boring anchovy toast – but the Saturday morning family ritual never changed. A pot of tea, two chocolate milkshakes, and egg and tomato sandwiches for three.

As teenagers (a new word – a new concept!) they'd met their friends at the popular milk bar at OK Bazaars, where they'd perch on barstools, hoping that the College boys would join them for ice-cream and chocolate sauce – with Horlicks sprinkled on top! – or Coke floats.

All this food... Alison's thoughts turned towards her own fridge.

Not now, warned Joey.

She's right! Not now! Alison grabbed a duster and began vigorously cleaning the pine bookshelves. When last had they been properly cleaned? Actually *doing* something made her feel better; at least the shelves would be clean when she re-filled them in the flat. Of course there'd be far fewer books after she'd got rid of most of them, so she'd be able to arrange the few remaining ornaments and vases between the books, just like in the 'beautiful homes' magazines. That would save space too!

Back to the bookshelf! Twins everywhere! The Bobbsey twins – *two* sets of twins; busy Mum! – the twins at St Clare's, and even twins at Malory Towers. No wonder her daughters had enjoyed those books so much. Alison knew that the Malory Towers books had been reprinted, with updated illustrations. How wonderful to have your books read by three generations!

She reached for her all-time favourites: the Dimsie books by Dorita Fairlie Bruce. (Dorita Fairlie Bruce… Alison loved the sound of her name, and the Bobbsey twins' creator was Laura Lee Hope – even better.) Was it time to pass the books on? She hesitated for a moment… Not yet, she'd hold onto them a while longer. She had a feeling that even Margie might agree with that. She'd compromise by giving away the books that she'd definitely not read again. Not many of those, but she was going to make a real effort – soon.

Anne of Green Gables… She'd laughed and cried with the residents of Avonlea… She was surprised to see that it had been written in 1908 – a true classic. (And yet another rhythmic-sounding author: Lucy Maud Montgomery…) Reprieve time for this one – Anne, Gilbert and their friends would stay. Mandy might enjoy them too… There was so much to re-read… Alison sighed contentedly. And how about a trip to Canada, taking in a visit to Prince Edward Island? Alison was sure she could find the house on which Green Gables had been modelled.

'All right, not yet,' she acceded to Joey's horrified stare – but for the moment she was enjoying the trip down fiction's memory lane.

Alison realised suddenly that the books she'd loved most had all been about girls she could identify with. Knights in armour and mythological gods and monsters hadn't gone down well – those books were still clean and untouched after all these years. Was it because of the stories themselves or was it the frightening illustrations? Either way, they could go. Smiling with satisfaction, she added several volumes, in excellent condition, to the Out-box. She was getting there.

In her teens she'd collected all the Georgette Heyer novels, her introduction to the historical romance, and here they all were... Thanks to them she'd felt quite at home the first time she wandered through the Park Lane area of London. She'd walked along the streets where her favourite characters had 'lived'. She looked lovingly at the books again and hesitatingly placed all but one, *Arabella*, in the Out-box. The print was very small and she'd never be able to read them again... After a brief mental battle she reluctantly added *Arabella* to the box.

What would a psychologist make of the books on the next shelf? Although the smell of disinfectant and the green walls of hospitals used to make her feel faint, she'd loved reading about the daily dramas of the nurses and young doctors in the Cherry Ames and Sue Barton books. Perhaps it was a result of her tennis-cum-hospital-watching schooldays! As she took the Sue Barton books off the shelf she noticed that they'd been written by Helen Dore Boylston – why did so many of those authors have three names, she wondered.

There were other books there, about children doing daring things that she would never have even contemplated. A boat trip on Durban Bay when she was ten had made her feel distinctly queasy, but in her imagination she'd sailed bravely with the Swallows and Amazons on their many adventures, and even flown 'on sorties' with Biggles. Despite her fear of heights (even the height of a horse) and of any animal larger than a dog, she'd mentally mucked out stables, groomed horses and delighted in the excitement of show jumping when she read the Pullein-Thompson books. There was a lot to be said for vicarious excitement – and all was well in the safety of her bedroom!

With a feeling of satisfaction, Alison placed all these offerings in the Out-box. She was making space, and someone else would enjoy the books – a double bonus! 'Where's the halo polish?' she asked Joey.

What next? *Veronica at the Wells*. Despite her lack of ballet talent – which her daughters had sadly inherited – she'd loved the 'Sadler's Wells' series. She'd been enthralled by the characters, who'd come to London from different backgrounds, all intent on becoming stars. Alison had shared in their problems and romances, and longed especially to see the Scottish countryside that Lorna Hill described so vividly. When she and Mark had visited Scotland for the first time it had all seemed so familiar to her – fiction had become reality! No wonder she'd thought of going to Canada to find the original Green Gables.

Where was her *Little Princesses*? Not fiction, but she'd treasured that book, written by Marion Crawford, aka Crawfie, governess to Princesses Elizabeth and Margaret. When Ally was very young, she and Margie had worn tartan skirts and twinsets just like the princesses, though of course not of the royal plaid! We wanted to be princesses too, Alison remembered, but that dream had soon faded.

So many princesses since then: Anne, Diana, and now Kate… 'Have I really lived through so many royal generations?' Alison was quite surprised. Despite the faded dreams of childhood, the fascination had lingered on. She and her friends had celebrated two recent royal weddings in style. For William and Kate there'd been scones with strawberry jam and cream, as well as sandwiches and frequent cups of tea; for Albert and Charlene of Monaco, koeksisters, éclairs and coffee. And champagne to toast both couples!

Joey turned away. *Enough now!*

Back to reality. Alison was astonished to see that the shelves were almost empty and the Out-box was overflowing.

Time for a little something. But even the grocery cupboard was almost bare. Just as well that she'd had a good breakfast; she'd go shopping later.

These Boots Are Made for Walkin'

That darn phone again!

'Di!' Alison was delighted to hear from her friend again.

'Pam and I are coming over tomorrow to share the pain of decluttering! Is that okay? It'll be fun!'

Alison's delight dissolved into apprehension.

Sharing is caring, muttered Joey sanctimoniously.

'We'll bring some snacks to keep us going through the day. See you tomorrow!'

'I love them both dearly,' Alison said to herself, 'but I don't think it's a good idea. Di will bulldoze me into doing whatever she wants!'

Just what you need, purred Joey.

They arrived early the next day in a chorus of enthusiasm, emptied some plastic containers onto the kitchen table and switched on the kettle.

'A quick coffee and croissant with jam before we get cracking! Where do we start?'

'The clothes, please,' asked Alison. 'I can't face that job.'

'That's why we're here!'

Di gasped as Alison opened her wardrobe. 'This may take longer than just today...'

'There's more in the spare room!' whispered Alison.

'Don't worry, Al, we'll do it together,' Pam tried to encourage her friend. Alison smiled nervously. Pam's efforts at dampening Di's overpowering enthusiasm had no effect.

'One cupboard at a time. Let the games begin!'

'Right! Please be seated while I present the Alison vintage selection,' said Di, holding an imaginary microphone.

She removed several hangers from the cupboard and dramatically presented a dress and jacket: 'Very fashionable before Noah's wife threw it overboard!'

'Nonsense! It was from Gina's wedding!'

'So? She's been married for at least twelve years.'

'But I like it!'

'When did you last wear it?'

'Can't remember.'

'When do you intend wearing it again?'

Silence...

'It'll come back into fashion some day,' Alison tried to defend herself.

'True, but you can always tell the revamped from the new, and after decades in the wardrobe,' she sniffed pointedly, 'the smell of mothballs is not alluring... Out!'

'I'm surprised you haven't got your wedding dress hidden away somewhere.' Di shook her head.

There was a long pause. 'Well, actually... I have.'

'What! Are you serious? I'd have thrown it out with the garbage! Out! Now! You will not wear it again! If you remarry – don't pull a face! – you'll definitely get a new one! And it won't be white meringue-style either!'

Alison reacted tearfully, 'You're acting like the television clothes police. I'm surprised you didn't bring their contraption that whisks one's clothes up and out of the room.'

'We should have!'

Pam intervened. 'Think about it, Alison. Rather concentrate on the happier memories.'

'Throw the wedding photos out at the same time,' cut in Di.

'No, *not* those,' Alison was adamant. 'Gina and Gemma will want them.'

'Oh, okay then.' Di's grudging voice made Alison feel guilty.

'It's so difficult...' Alison sighed.

'That's why we're here,' comforted Pam.

'From Alison's dark period,' explained Di holding up three skirts, one navy, one dark grey, and one bottle green. 'Oh happy day!' she sang. 'How you must have brightened the schoolgirls' lives in those dismal classrooms!'

Alison giggled. 'There's quite a story about that green skirt. I wore it on my first day at Barnsleigh High – I'd carefully chosen a no-nonsense dark green skirt, and a white blouse, so that I wouldn't stand out.'

'And what happened?' Pam asked.

'My entrance was a bit like a Leon Schuster film. I walked into the assembly hall, and there were hundreds of girls wearing dark green skirts and white blouses. Talk about blending into the community! I'd been interviewed by phone so I'd never even seen the school uniform.'

'And you've *kept* it! I don't believe it!' Di was incredulous. 'Out with them all!'

For once Alison didn't object.

Di returned to the wardrobe. 'No wonder you're always late. Burrowing in here to find clothes that aren't creased after being squashed together for at least a quarter of a century. Unbelievable...'

'Never mind the insults,' pacified Pam. 'Wait until we've finished! You won't know yourself, Ally, with your small, wearable twenty-first century range!'

'And no more contributions from *ouma se doos*,' added Di.

'Come on, Di,' Pam defended Alison. 'I bet even you have some things from the old days.'

'Nothing like this!' Di shifted her gaze to the cupboard floor. 'And what's all that mess down there?'

'My handbags, of course,' replied Alison proudly.

'A bag for every colour and occasion?'

'Yes,' she said defiantly. 'You know there was a time when we had to have shoes and handbags to match our clothes.'

'And that time is long, long gone,' Di chipped in instantly.

'Ally, these days one has one bag for everything,' Pam explained patiently. 'Look at mine here, and Di's too. I do have a more formal one for evening and a sportsbag for the gym – but that's it. You don't need so many.'

Di continued, relentless: 'What about having a garage sale – like in the *Clean House* TV programme? We could all go on a cruise to Mauritius with the proceeds! Come on, Ally – choose a few bags that you can't live without. Then we'll sort out the shoes.'

She opened the shoe drawer. 'Alison! A rival for Imelda Marcos. Since when did you have a thing about shoes?'

'I don't "have a thing" about them! I just can't throw them away.' Alison felt even more deflated.

'We'll do it for you! Oh my goodness, look at these! Pointed toes are back in fashion but not these winkle-pickers of our youth!'

Di tossed off her sandals and tried on the offending pair. 'Only a man could have enticed us to voluntarily ruin our feet in shoes like these! And only women would torture themselves for the sake of fashion. How stupid we were! Anyone whose toes grew in this shape would make medical history – they'd be taken around the world like the Elephant Man! It's only the orthopaedic surgeons who are happy about these weird fashions.'

Pam and Alison exchanged glances. Di was off on one of her hobbyhorses…

'Bring me your broken, your heel-less, your scuffed and your outdated models,' declaimed Di. 'Throw them out – *now*! You could open a fancy dress hire shop with this lot.' She started stuffing the shoes into the box.

'No, wait. I've got a better idea,' said Pam. 'I'm sure that the university drama department would grab your museum pieces for their historical wardrobe section.'

Hysterical, more likely, commented Joey.

'They might even name the collection after you!'

'Very funny.' Alison was not amused.

'Do you remember that poem we learnt at junior school?' Di was undeterred. '"New shoes, new shoes; red and pink and blue shoes"? I think you took that poem too seriously.'

Alison grabbed a sandal and threw it at Di, who caught it and replied, more gently this time, 'Malign me as much as you like Ally! But do you have cupboard space for all this stuff in the flat?'

Alison shook her head.

'Well, there's your answer.' Di turned back to the cupboard.

'Are you taking part in *Strictly Come Dancing*? How many pairs of silver sandals does anyone need? Stiletto heels, *nogal*! From what I've noticed, we're all into the "comfort before glamour" stage. You – do – not – need – these.'

'Ja, it's one of the joys of getting old,' smiled Pam.

'Older, not old,' corrected Di! 'It's all in the mind.'

'Actually, in the feet,' giggled Alison.

This broke the rather tense atmosphere and they all collapsed onto the bed in fits of laughter.

When they'd recovered, Alison examined the remaining shoes. 'Some of the really high ones belong to the girls.'

'Well, return them then! Or ask them if you can give them away. They probably won't even know what shoes you're talking about – they'd have collected them a long time ago if they'd wanted them.'

Pam, seeing Alison's downcast look, gave her a hug. 'I know it's awful going through all this, Al, but it really has to be done. You'll be so pleased afterwards.'

Alison smiled weakly.

Di disdainfully held up a pair of walking shoes. 'Are these holy soles from your religious period? No self-respecting jumble sale would take these, Ally! These must be the original takkies from before North Stars and Nikes.'

Di paused, but only briefly. 'Don't tell me! You couldn't bear to throw them away! You obviously aren't a member of the "One In One Out" club!'

'I think it's time for a break,' said Pam. 'I could do with some more coffee.'

Harmony was restored as they caught up with family news.

Alison cheered up: 'At least I'll be helping Mandy with her project. Let's get back to work.'

They returned to the bedroom.

Di reached up to the top shelf of the wardrobe. 'What's this? A hatbox! A *hatbox*! When did you last see one of these, ladies? Straight from Paris, or maybe Parys! Come on! When did you last wear a hat, Ally? What a pity there's no film studio here. You'd make a fortune from renting these extraordinary relics!'

'I think you're most unkind. These all mean something to me,' said Alison. 'That was my gran's hatbox.'

'I know what; we'll take some photos so you can look at them whenever you really miss them,' promised Pam.

'Or you could start a shop called Hats Galore!' suggested Di.

'And *this*?' Di draped a grey cloche around her head and posed languidly: 'Greta Garbo. I vont to be alone.'

Alison stood her ground: 'I wore that to the July when Mark and I were just getting serious. You had to have something special at the biggest horserace of the year! And in any case I think it's rather nice. It doesn't take up much space; I want to keep it.'

'Have you really kept it since before you were engaged?' Pam sounded really surprised. 'You really should get rid of it now.'

Di was on a roll. 'Ladies! Here's the original Easter bonnet! All aboard for the Easter Parade! You could put it on the coffee table as a substitute for your floral arrangement!'

'Come on Di; this isn't easy for her.' Pam was watching Alison's face.

'At least I haven't kept any of those ghastly maternity dresses, gathered under the bust to accentuate the bulging tum,' said Alison defensively.

Unfazed, Di grabbed Alison's fruit bowl and placed it on her head, holding it gingerly. 'And here we have an original Carmen Miranda fruit salad!'

How suitable, thought Joey. *They're all nutty and fruity.*

'This straw hat must have looked good when you bought it… "Very pleasing, modom, but I'm afraid that the moth-eaten ribbon and the broken straw won't quate appeal to the contemporary buyer!"'

Excited by her creativity, Di grabbed another hat, leaned against the cupboard, crossed her legs, opened an imaginary umbrella and burst into *Singing in the Rain*! 'The original Gene Kelly fedora? Please tell us when you wore *that*? A fancy dress party?'

'It's not so old-fashioned. Britney Spears wore one to…'

Nothing was stopping Di. 'And here, ladies, straight from the 'sixties! An original Jackie Kennedy pillbox!'

Alison sighed. 'You're right, Di. But they were so fashionable…'

'I'm surprised you haven't got a real Ascot hat in your collection! I think you've kept everything else.'

'Ascot hats, weren't they wonderful?' smiled Pam.

'Wonderful in *My Fair Lady*, yes – but not in a Durban suburban wardrobe!'

Di was off once again: 'Ta-da! From the Royal wardrobe, with the original net roses and veil!' Di curtsied, struggling to keep the hat from falling over her face.

'How did the Queen Mum cope?' Pam wondered.

'"Quite fetching, ma'am. Just the thing for the Royal garden party!" No! Out with the lot!' shouted Di, pointing determinedly to the rapidly filling Out-box.

She looked back at the wardrobe, to see what was next in the firing line. She looked again. They were done! 'We're done! Can you believe it!'

'Phew,' gasped Alison and Pam in unison.

'Lunch time!' said Alison, glad that the job was over.

'Okay, let's heat up my tuna lasagne,' said Pam. 'And Di's brought your favourite lemon meringue pie. Let's celebrate!'

'We've actually done quite well – I can close the wardrobe door now! Thanks, girls. I could never have done this without you. To be perfectly honest I was really nervous when you said you were coming to help me. And it's all worked so well.'

'"That's what friends are for",' Pam hummed softly.

It's a Lovely Day Today!

Margie had stayed overnight, helping sort out last-minute hassles, and uncharacteristically refraining from comment. The removal van was ready to leave with the furniture and boxes. Margie and Alison's cars were piled dangerously high with clothes, the smaller In-boxes and pot plants. The photos and papers for Mandy's project were safely stowed in the boot. A very disgruntled cat was sitting in a basket on the front seat.

'Well done, Al! You've finally made it! Decluttering wasn't so bad after all!'

'You're right, Margie! It was a piece of cake!'

The Recipes

Thanks to my family and friends for all the cakes that saved my sanity, if not my waistline, during my decluttering nightmare—Alison

Note
Most of these recipes date back to pre-metric days:
1 teaspoon (tsp) = 5 ml
1 tablespoon (Tbs) = 15 ml
1 cup = 250 ml

Aunt Ann's Ginger Loaf

- Sift and combine the following ingredients:
  3 cups flour
  1 tsp baking powder
  ¾ cup castor sugar
  3 tsp ground ginger
  2 tsp mixed spice
  2 tsp bicarbonate of soda

- Make a well in the centre and add the following:
  3 eggs, beaten lightly
  1 cup oil
  1 cup golden syrup
  1 cup warm water

- Beat all with an electric beater or wooden spoon (not a food processor).
- Grease/spray 1 large loaf tin, or 2 small loaf tins, leaving plenty of room for rising.
- Bake at 180°C for 1 hour.
- Remove from oven and after 5 minutes turn out onto a wire rack to cool.

Kathy's Mum's Nutty Date Biscuits

Have ready the following ingredients:
    455 g dates, chopped
    1 cup pecan nuts, chopped
    5 Tbs flour
    ¾ cup sugar
    3 eggs
    1 tsp vanilla essence
    1 tsp baking powder

- Mix all the dry ingredients and add the chopped dates and nuts.
- Add the vanilla essence and the beaten eggs.
- Place the mixture in a greased tin.
- Bake at 220°C for 15 to 20 minutes – until firm.
- Cut into squares while still hot.

Mum's Cheese Cake — for every occasion, special or not!

BASE
¾–1 packet Marie biscuits
125 g melted butter or margarine

- Crush the biscuits and thoroughly mix with the melted butter.
- Press onto the base and sides of an ovenproof dish.

FILLING
500 g cream cheese
2 eggs
4 Tbs cream
1 tsp cornflour
5 Tbs sugar
pinch salt

METHOD
- Mix the cornflour into the cream, making sure there are no lumps.
- Combine all ingredients and mix by hand.
- Spoon into base.
- Bake at 160°C for 30 minutes.
- Turn off oven and leave the cake inside for a few minutes.
- Then open oven door and leave for a few minutes more.

Pam's Grated Chocolate Cake

You will need:

    200 g slab of nut chocolate – grated, but not too finely;
        it must have small choc chunks!
    ¾ cup sugar
    ½ cup oil
    1 cup flour
    1 + 3 tsp baking powder
    4 eggs
    ½ cup warm water

- Sift the flour, then mix in the sugar.
- Separate the eggs.
- Beat the egg whites with 1 tsp baking powder. Set aside.
- Add the egg yolks, oil and water to dry ingredients.
- Add the grated chocolate, then the 3 tsps baking powder.
- Fold in the egg whites.
- Put the mixture into a cake tin.
- Bake at 180°C for 45 minutes.

Zoë's Red Velvet Cupcakes

- Cream together:
  250 g butter
  1 heaped cup castor sugar

- Add:
  250 ml buttermilk
  50 ml white vinegar
  10 ml vanilla essence
  2 jumbo eggs
  10 ml cocoa
  30 ml red food colouring

- Sift together and mix in:
  2½ cups flour
  5 ml bicarbonate of soda

- Spoon into cupcake cases placed in muffin tins, so that each is about two-thirds full.
- Bake at 180°C for about 20 minutes.

Makes 30 cupcakes.

Aunt Hetty's Fruit Cake

INGREDIENTS
   500 g mixed cake fruit
   1 cup sugar
   120 g butter
   1 cup water
   1 tsp bicarbonate of soda
   2 cups flour
   1 egg, beaten lightly

Those are the basic ingredients; you can jazz it up with:
   nuts
   spices
   glacé cherries
   brandy

METHOD
- In a large pot (for later) – boil together for 10 minutes the fruit (but not the cherries), water and sugar. Allow to cool a bit and then add the bicarb in a little water (it should fizz).
- Add the flour, then the egg. Then the rest.
- Put all into a cake tin lined with plenty of layers of cooking paper (I do four layers).
- Cover with foil and bake for 1½ hours at 150°C.
- Allow to cool before taking it out of the baking tin.

Ally's Fruit Slices

- Make a rich pastry with:
  250 g flour
  2 tsp baking powder
  150 g butter
  100 g sugar
  1 tsp vanilla essence
  1 egg

- Grease a baking tin, about A4 size (not bigger). Squash the dough into a flattish lump and then press it down to cover the whole base and sides of the tin, taking care to thin it out at the corners. Trim the top edge with a sharp knife.

FOR FILLING:
  1 cup sugar
  1 cup roughly chopped walnuts (not too fine)
  1 cup sultanas
  1 egg
  1 Tbs butter

- Cream the butter, sugar and egg. Add the sultanas and nuts.
- Spread the mixture over the pastry.
- Cover with foil and bake at 190°C for about 30 minutes.
- Remove foil and if it looks a bit anaemic put it back without the foil for a couple of minutes.
- Cut into slices/squares when cool.
- Serve hot or cold; on its own or with cream or plain yoghurt.

Variation: use dates and almonds instead of sultanas and walnuts.

Margie's Carrot Cake

- Set the oven to 160°C.
- Grease and flour a chiffon cake tin.
  *A chiffon tin? What's that? ***

INGREDIENTS – CAKE
   2 cups sifted cake flour
   1½ cups castor sugar
   2 tsp cinnamon
   ½ tsp salt
   1 tsp bicarbonate of soda
   1 tsp baking powder
   1–1½ tsp ground ginger
   3 eggs, extra large
   ½ Tbs vanilla essence
   1½ cups oil
   ½ cup of tinned crushed pineapple, drained and squeezed
   2 cups finely grated carrots, squeezed dry
   1 cup pecan nuts, roughly chopped (keep some back for
   decorating the icing)

- Sift together all the dry ingredients.
- Make a well in the centre and add the eggs, vanilla essence
  and oil. Beat well.
- By hand fold in the pineapple, carrots and nuts.
- Pour into prepared baking tin.
- Bake at 160°C about 50 minutes. Test with a skewer.
- Turn off oven and leave cake for 10 minutes.
- Remove from oven and allow to cool for 20 minutes.
- Gently loosen and turn out onto cooling rack.

---

* Joey, it's one of those cake tins with a funnel in the middle. I use a floppy
  silicone one – and the cake just falls out in one piece!

INGREDIENTS – ICING
   60 g butter
   60 g firm cream cheese
   250 g icing sugar
   ½ tsp vanilla essence

- Cream butter and icing sugar. Very gently stir in the cream cheese and vanilla.
- Spread over the cake and decorate with the reserved nuts.

Aunt Becky's Apple Cake

- Cream together:
  1 egg
  ¾ cup sugar
  60 g melted butter

- Stir in:
  1½ cups flour
  2 tsp baking powder
  pinch of salt
  ½ cup milk

- Spread all into a greased pie dish.
- Add 1 tin of pie apples, and push down into the mixture.
- Sprinkle with 2 Tbs sugar mixed with 1 tsp cinnamon.
- Bake at 180°C for 50 minutes.
- Serve with cream or custard for tea or dessert!

Alison's variations: Substitute tinned apricots or peaches. Drain, and dry on paper towels.
Mix apple and apricot for a great sweet 'n sour flavour.

Miffie's Milk Tart

Recipe may be doubled.

INGREDIENTS
   275 ml milk
   3 Tbs flour
   1¼ tsp cornflour
   90 ml sugar (castor might be good)
   2 eggs, separated
   1 tsp vanilla essence
   *sweet pastry for base

- Mix flour, cornflour and a generous Tbs of the sugar.
- Add a little of the milk and the flavouring, and stir well to make a smooth paste.
- Boil the rest of the milk and gradually add the mixture to it (first add some of the milk to the flour mixture).
- Boil again, taking care not to overheat, till of a smooth, firm consistency.
- Allow to cool a little and add the egg yolks, beaten with a further 1 Tbs of the sugar.
- Beat the egg whites with the rest of the sugar, and fold in.
- Pour into a flan dish lined with fairly thin sweet pastry*, and bake at 190°C until it browns – about 25 mins.
- When cool, sprinkle with cinnamon.

Serve at room temperature.

---

* You could use the rich pastry recipe from Ally's Fruit Slices on page 143.
OR
* Make a biscuit base, by thoroughly crunching up about 120 g Marie biscuits (or similar) and mixing with about 4 or 5 tablespoons of melted butter.

Bianca's Biscotti: Ciambelle Romane

Recipe may be halved.

- Mix:
  500 g self-raising flour
  125 g sugar
  pinch salt
  2 heaped Tbs aniseed

- Separately, mix:
  125 g oil
  125 g wine (white or red)

- Combine all and roll the dough out flat.
- Cut into large rounds then cut out smaller rounds from inside the large ones.*
- Bake at 170°C for 20 to 30 minutes.

Makes 45 to 50 biscotti. Good with coffee!

---

* *Notes from me (Alison)*: If you haven't got suitable biscuit cutters use a tumbler top and a washed-out Berocca tube!
You can squash the remaining middle bits together and make some more. And just bake the last little bit separately, and eat it yourself!

Zoë's Scones

Really different – fun and easy to make!

INGREDIENTS
  1 tin Sprite (or similar lemon-lime flavoured fizzy drink)
  250 g cream
  500 g self-raising flour
  pinch of salt

- Mix all together.
- Spoon into greased/sprayed cookie tins, so that each is about two-thirds full.
- Bake at 180°C for 20+ minutes.

Di's Lemon Meringue Pie

CRUST
 1 packet Marie biscuits
 125 g butter

FILLING
 4 egg yolks
 3 Tbs lemon juice
 1 tin condensed milk
 pinch salt

MERINGUE
 4 egg whites
 8 Tbs sugar
 pinch salt
 a few drops of vanilla essence

METHOD
- Crush the biscuits.
- Melt the butter and mix thoroughly with the crumbs.
- Line a pie dish with the biscuit mixture and refrigerate.
- Beat all the filling ingredients together until thick, and pour into the base.

- Beat the egg whites until stiff, and add the sugar, one tablespoon at a time.
- Add a pinch of salt and a few drops of vanilla essence.
- Spoon the meringue on top of the filling and swirl into peaks.

- Bake at 130°C for about 45 minutes.

Mandy's No-Bake Marie Biscuit Balls

For Gran, for your help with my project!

 1 packet crushed Marie biscuits
 250 g melted butter
 500 g icing sugar
 2 beaten eggs
 2 tsp vanilla essence
 4 tsp cocoa

- Mix all ingredients together and put the mixture into the fridge.
- When it's cold roll it into balls.
- Roll the balls in crushed nuts or desiccated coconut.